"You lured me here on false pretenses. You had no right."

"You knew I was the kind of man who would never forgive...." He took a step closer. "You forced my hand over the check. That stung my pride."

"Your pride!" Frances scoffed.

His voice changed, became harder. "The ruler of a country must be a man of pride. If not, he is unfit to rule. I could not allow an insult to go unpunished. I decided it was time you had a lesson in reality."

"Reality?" she echoed, hardly able to believe her ears. "Putting me with your concubines? Ali, this has gone far enough. I want my bag, my clothes, and I want to get out of here."

He laughed softly. "You are wonderful. You are completely helpless in my power and yet you speak with such authority. I tremble in my shoes."

"I don't believe this," she said in a shaking voice. "I'm dreaming, and I'll wake up soon."

"I wish you the sweetest of dreams, and I hope they will all be of me. But when you awake, you will still be here. And you will remain here, at my pleasure, until I decide otherwise."

Lucy Gordon cut her writing teeth on magazine journalism, interviewing many of the world's most interesting men, including Warren Beatty, Richard Chamberlain, Roger Moore, Sir Alec Guinness and Sir John Gielgud. She also camped out with lions in Africa, and had many other unusual experiences, which have often provided the background for her books.

She is married to a Venetian, whom she met while on holiday in Venice. They got engaged within two days, and have now been married for twenty-five years. They live in the Midlands of the U.K., with their dogs.

Two of her books have won the Romance Writers of America RITA Award—*Song of the Lorelei* in 1990, and *His Brother's Child* in 1998 in the Best Traditional Romance category.

Books by Lucy Gordon

HARLEQUIN ROMANCE®
3561—FARELLI'S WIFE
3596—RICO'S SECRET CHILD

THE SHEIKH'S REWARD
Lucy Gordon

TORONTO • NEW YORK • LONDON
AMSTERDAM • PARIS • SYDNEY • HAMBURG
STOCKHOLM • ATHENS • TOKYO • MILAN • MADRID
PRAGUE • WARSAW • BUDAPEST • AUCKLAND

ISBN 0-373-03634-5

THE SHEIKH'S REWARD

First North American Publication 2000.

CHAPTER ONE

HE WAS a prince to his fingertips. Tall, black-haired, his head set at a proud angle, Prince Ali Ben Saleem, Sheikh of the principality of Kamar, drew everyone's gaze as he walked into the casino.

It wasn't just his handsome features and his tall body with its combination of power and grace. There was something about him that seemed to proclaim him skilful at everything he attempted. And so men regarded him with envy, women with interest.

Frances Callam watched with the others, but her eyes held a peculiar intentness. Ali Ben Saleem was the man she had come here to study.

She was a freelance journalist, much in demand for her skill at profiling people. Editors knew that she was unbeatable in stories where large sums of money were concerned. And Ali was one of the wealthiest men in the world.

'Will you look at that?' Joey Baines breathed in awe, watching Ali's imperial progress to the tables. Joey was a private detective whom she sometimes hired as an assistant. She'd brought him along tonight as cover while she visited the casino and watched Ali at play.

'I'm looking,' Fran murmured. 'He certainly lives up to the legend, doesn't he? In appearance anyway.'

'What's the rest of the legend?'

'He's a law unto himself, accountable to nobody for where his money comes from or where it goes to.'

'But we know where it comes from,' Joey objected.
'Those oil wells he's got gushing away in the desert.'

'And a lot of it vanishes in places like this,' Fran
said, looking around her with disapproval.

'Hey, Fran, lighten up. Can't we enjoy life among
the fleshpots for just one night? It's in a good cause.'

'It's in the cause of nailing a man who doesn't like
answering questions about himself, and finding out
what he has to hide,' Fran said firmly.

Joey ran a finger around the inside of his collar. His
short, undistinguished person looked uncomfortable in
the black tie and dinner jacket that was *de rigueur* for
the men.

'I can't believe you came here looking like a god-
dess just to work,' he said, eyeing her slender figure,
pale skin and red-gold hair with wistful lust.

'Down, Fido,' Fran said amiably. 'Tonight this is
my work outfit. I need to look as if I belong in this
place.'

She'd succeeded in her aim. Her dress seemed to be
solid gold glitter with a neckline that plunged low, and
a side slit that came up to her thigh. She was rather
disconcerted by the dress's frank immodesty, and had
hired it only with misgiving. But she was glad now
that she'd done so. In the glittering, sophisticated am-
bience of The Golden Chance, London's premier casino, this was how to look.

As well as the dress, she'd hired the solid gold jew-
ellery that went with it. Hanging earrings accentuated
the length of her neck, heavy gold bracelets weighed
down her wrists, and a long gold pendant plunged between her breasts, emphasising her *décolletage*.

I look like a kept woman, she thought, faintly
shocked at herself.

But so did every other woman here, and in that respect the outfit was a success.

Certainly she could have held her own among the women who crowded around Sheikh Ali, competing for his attention, and being rewarded with a smile, or a kiss of the fingers in their direction. The sight made her seethe.

'Arrogant so-and-so,' she muttered. 'Men like that are supposed to be extinct.'

'Only the ones who can't get away with it,' Joey told her wisely. 'Those who can are as bad as ever.'

'You're jealous,' she said indignantly.

'We all are, Fran! Look around you. Every man in the place wants to be him, and every woman wants to sleep with him.'

'Not every one,' she said firmly. 'Not me.'

Ali had finished his royal progress and was settling at one of the tables. Fran edged nearer, trying to observe him without looking too interested.

He played for very high stakes, and when he lost he merely shrugged. Fran gulped at the sums he tossed away as though they were nothing. She noticed, too, that once play started he forgot about the women at his elbow. One minute he was flirting madly with them. The next they didn't exist. Her annoyance grew.

It grew even more when play stopped and he turned on the charm again, clearly expecting to take up with them where he'd left off. Worse still, they let him.

'You see that?' she muttered to Joey. 'Why doesn't one of them spit in his eye?'

'You try spitting in the eye of a hundred billion,' Joey said. 'See how easy it is. Why must you be such a puritan, Fran?'

'I can't help it. It's how I was raised. It's not decent

for one man to have so much—so much—just so much.'

She'd been going to say 'so much money', but Sheikh Ali had so much of everything. From the moment of his birth it had all fallen into his lap. His father, the late Sheikh Saleem, had married an Englishwoman and remained faithful to her all his life. Ali was their only son.

He'd inherited his little principality at the age of twenty-one. His first act had been to cancel all deals with the world's mighty oil corporations, and to renegotiate them, giving Kamar a far larger slice of the profits. The companies had raged but given in. Kamar's oil was of priceless quality.

In the ten years since then he'd multiplied his country's wealth more than ten times. He lived a charmed life between two worlds. He had apartments in both London and New York, and he commuted between them in his private jet, making huge, complex deals.

When not enjoying the high life in the west he returned to his domain to live in one of his palaces, or to visit Wadi Sita, a top secret retreat in the desert, where he was reputed to indulge in all manner of excesses. He never contradicted these rumours, nor even deigned to acknowledge them, and because no journalist had ever been allowed to glimpse the truth the stories flourished unchecked.

'Does Howard know you're here tonight?' Joey asked, naming the man whom Fran usually dated.

'Of course not. He'd never approve. In fact he doesn't approve of my doing this story. I asked him what he could tell me about Ali, and he just gave me the PR line about how important he was, and how Kamar was a valuable ally. When I said there were too many mysteries, Howard went pale and said, ''For pity's sake, don't offend him.'''

'What a wimp!' Joey said provocatively.

'Howard isn't a wimp, but he is a merchant banker, and he has a banker's priorities.'

'And you're going to marry this guy?'

'I never said that,' Fran answered quickly. 'Probably. One day. Maybe.'

'Boy, you're really head over heels about him, aren't you?'

'Can we concentrate on what we're here for?' she asked frostily.

'Place your bets, please!'

Ali pushed a large stake out over the board to red twenty-seven, then leaned back with an air of supreme indifference. He maintained it throughout the spinning of the wheel as the little ball bounced merrily from red to black, from one number to another. Fran found she was holding her breath, her eyes riveted on the wheel, until at last it stopped.

Red twenty-two.

The croupier raked the stakes in. Fran watched Sheikh Ali, frowning. He didn't even look at the fortune that was vanishing. All his attention was for his new stake.

Suddenly he looked up at her.

She gasped. Two points of light pierced her, held her imprisoned.

Then he smiled, and it was the most wickedly charming smile she had ever seen. It invited her into a conspiracy of delight and something in her leaped to accept. She discovered that she was smiling back; she didn't know how or why. Simply that the smile had taken over her mouth, then her eyes, then her whole body.

Common sense told her that only pure chance had made him look in her direction, but somehow she didn't believe it. He'd sensed her there. Among so many others, he'd known that she was watching him, and been impelled to meet her eyes.

Ali leaned forward to her, stretching out his hand across the narrow table. As if hypnotised she placed her own slender hand in his. He held it for a moment and she had the unnerving sense of steely strength in those long fingers. There was power enough there to break a man—or a woman.

Then he raised her hand to his lips. Fran drew in a sharp breath as his mouth brushed her skin. It was the lightest touch, but it was enough for her to sense the whole male animal, vibrant, sensual, dangerous.

'Place your bets, please.'

He released her, reached for his stake and pushed it out onto the table. It stopped at black twenty-two, but he didn't look to see. He'd forgotten the other women as soon as the wheel spun, but he kept his eyes on Fran, ignoring the wheel. She watched him back, meaning to tear her eyes away, but mysteriously unable to do so.

Black twenty-two.

Ali seemed to come out of a dream to realise that the croupier was pushing the chips towards him. It had been a large stake and with one win he'd recouped almost all his losses. He grinned, showing white teeth, and indicated the place beside him with the slightest inclination of his head.

She edged around the table towards him. The other

women pouted and sulked, reluctant to give way to her, but he dismissed them with a faint gesture.

Fran felt as if she was moving in a dream. Luck had fallen her way with stunning suddenness. She had meant to study Ali tonight, and now fate had presented her with the perfect opportunity.

'You have brought me luck,' he said as she reached him and sat down. 'Now you must stay close by me so that my luck remains.'

'Surely you're not superstitious?' she asked with a smile. 'Your luck will come and go. It has nothing to do with me.'

'I think otherwise,' he pronounced in a tone that silenced further argument. 'The spell you cast is for me alone. Not for any other man. Remember that.'

Arrogant beast, she thought. If this didn't happen to suit me I'd enjoy taking him down a peg.

'Place your bets.'

With a gesture of his hand Ali indicated for her to place the stake for him. She put the counters on red fifteen, and held her breath as the wheel spun.

Red fifteen.

A sigh went up from everyone around the table.

Almost everyone.

Ali alone was not watching. His eyes were fixed admiringly on Fran. As the counters were pushed towards him he gave a shrug which said, 'Of course.'

'I don't believe that happened,' she breathed.

'You made it happen,' he assured her, 'and you will make it happen again.'

'No, it was chance. You should stop now. Take it while you have it.'

His smile said that it was for petty men to worry about such things. Princes controlled their own fate.

Under his hypnotic glance Fran found herself believing it.

'Put it on for me again,' he said. 'All of it.'

Dazed, she piled up all his winnings and went to put them on—on—

'I can't decide,' she said frantically.

'What day of the month is your birthday?'

'The twenty-third.'

'Red or black? Choose.'

'Black,' she said recklessly.

'Then black twenty-three it is.'

She watched in agony as the wheel began to spin.

'Don't look,' he said, smiling. 'Look only at me, and let the little gods of the tables take care of the matter.'

'Can you make them do your pleasure as well?' she whispered.

'I can make anyone and anything do my pleasure,' he said simply.

The wheel stopped.

Black twenty-three.

A prickle went up Fran's spine. This was eerie. Ali saw her startled look and laughed.

'Witchcraft,' he said. 'And you are the most beautiful witch of all.'

'I—I don't believe it,' she stammered. 'It can't happen like that.'

'It happened because you are magic. And I can't resist magic.'

On the words he dropped his head and laid his lips against her palm. Instantly Fran felt as though she was being scorched, although the touch of his lips was teasingly soft. The sensation started in her skin and swiftly pervaded her. She had a sense of alarm and would have snatched her hand back, but she remembered in time that such gaucheness wouldn't fit the role she was playing. She smiled, hoping she looked as though such tributes happened every day.

The croupier pushed over the winnings. 'I'll take them,' Ali announced.

A man standing behind his chair counted up and wrote the total on a piece of paper. Fran gasped as she saw it.

While the man went to cash the chips Ali rose and drew Fran away from the table. 'Now we will dine together,' he announced.

Fran hesitated. Ancient female wisdom told her that it wasn't clever to accept such an abrupt invitation from a man she'd known barely half an hour. But she was in pursuit of a story, and she wouldn't succeed by refusing the first real break she'd been given. Besides, a restaurant was public enough.

Out of the corner of her eye she saw Joey, his jaw dropping. She gave him a wink and swept out on Ali's arm.

His Rolls-Royce was waiting outside, the chauffeur already standing with the door open. Ali handed her gallantly inside. The chauffeur got in and started the car without waiting for instructions.

When they were moving Ali turned to her, smiling mischievously, and reached into his pockets. From one he produced a necklace of priceless pearls, from the other, a diamond necklace.

'Which?' he asked.

'Whi—?'

'One of them is yours. Take your pick.'

She gaped. He carried such things around with him, in his pockets?

Feeling as though she'd been transported to another planet, she said, 'I'll take the diamonds.' The voice didn't sound like her own.

'Turn your neck so that I can remove that gold pendant,' he commanded. 'The man who gives you such trumpery baubles doesn't know how to value you.'

His fingers brushed her neck, and she took a shuddering, uncontrollable breath. This wasn't how the evening was supposed to go. She'd come prepared to analyse Sheikh Ali, to dislike and despise him. But she hadn't come prepared to be overwhelmed by him. It had simply happened.

She felt the chill on her flesh as he draped a king's ransom in diamonds about her neck. His fingertips brushed against her nape and she had to struggle not to tremble at that soft, devastating impact. Then there was another sensation, so light that she couldn't be sure of it. Had he kissed the back of her neck or not? How dared he? If he had…

'They were made for you,' he declared, turning her to face him. 'No woman has ever looked better in diamonds.'

'And you speak from a wide experience?' she said demurely.

He laughed, neither offended nor ashamed. 'Wider than you can imagine,' he assured her. 'But tonight none of the others exist. There is only you in the world. Now tell me your name.'

'My name—' She had a sudden inspiration. 'My name is Diamond.'

His eyes lit up. 'You have wit. Excellent. That will do for now. Before the night is over you will tell me your real name.'

He held her left hand in both of his and studied the fingers.

'No rings,' he observed. 'You are neither married nor promised, unless you are one of those modern women who scorn to tell the world that you belong to a man. Or maybe you scorn to let yourself belong?'

'I belong to no man,' she said. 'I belong to myself, and no man will ever own me.'

'Then you have never known love. When you do, you'll find that your aloof ideas mean nothing. When you love, you will give, and it must be all of yourself, or the gift means nothing.'

'And who do you belong to?' she demanded with spirit.

He laughed. 'That is quite another matter. But I could say that I belong to a million people.' Kamar had a population of one million. 'No part of my life is entirely my own. Even my heart is not mine to give. Tell me about the little man with you. I wondered if he might have been your lover.'

'Would that have made any difference to you?'

'None at all, since he made no effort to protect you from me. A man who cannot hold onto his woman is no man.'

'Do I need protecting from you?' Fran mused, teasing him with her eyes.

He laid his lips against her hand. 'I wonder if we'll discover that we each need protection from the other?' he said thoughtfully.

'Who knows?' she murmured, replying as she felt her role required. 'The pleasure will come in discovering.'

'And you are a woman made for pleasure.'

Fran drew a slow breath, shocked at how much the

words affected her. She was used to hearing her brains praised. Howard admired her looks but was just as likely to acclaim her common sense. And her common sense told her that, while passion mattered, it wasn't the whole of life. Suddenly she was no longer sure of that.

He listened to her silence and added, 'You're not going to pretend not to know what I mean.'

'There are many kinds of pleasure,' she fenced.

'Not for us. For you and I there is only one kind— the pleasure to be shared by a man and a woman in the heat of desire.'

'Isn't it a little soon to be thinking of desire?'

'We were thinking of desire the moment our eyes met. Don't try to deny it.'

She couldn't have begun to deny it. The truth was shocking but it was still the truth. She wondered wildly if she could jump out of the car and flee, but he was holding her hand in a grip that was only superficially gentle. Underneath, it was unbreakable.

He touched her face with his fingertips. The next thing she knew, his lips were on hers in the lightest kiss she'd ever known. It was so light that it might not have happened, except that it was followed by another on her chin, her jaw, her eyes, and again on her lips. She barely felt them, but she felt their effects in the tingling excitement they produced all over her body.

This was alarming. If he'd tried to overwhelm her with power she could have defended herself. But Sheikh Ali was an artist, putting out all his artistry to bring her under his spell. And there seemed to be no defence against that.

She moved helplessly against him, neither returning his kisses nor fending him off. He looked down into her face, but it was too dark in the car for him to find what he wanted to know. Nor could she see the little frown of uncertainty between his eyes.

The long, sleek car glided to a halt in a quiet street in London's most exclusive area. Slowly he released her. The chauffeur opened the door and Ali took her hand to assist her out. Then she was stepping out onto the pavement, and realising what she ought to have thought of before—that he had brought her not to a restaurant but to his home.

She knew this was the moment when she should act sensibly and run, but what kind of journalist ran away at the first hint of danger?

She gave herself a little shake. Of course there was no danger. What had put that thought into her head?

The tall windows of the mansion were filled with light. One on the ground floor had the curtains pulled back, revealing crystal chandeliers and lavish furnishings.

Slowly the front door opened. A tall man in Arab robes and headdress stood there massively.

'Welcome to my humble home,' said Prince Ali Ben Saleem.

CHAPTER TWO

As SHE entered the house Fran blinked at her gorgeous
surroundings. She was in a large hallway, dominated
by a huge, sweeping staircase, and with double doors
on either side. There were exotic tiles beneath her feet,
and more of them covering the walls. It was bewil-
dering but gorgeous.

Every set of doors leading off the hall was closed,
but at that moment one pair was thrown open and a
man emerged. He approached Ali, not appearing to
notice Fran, and addressed him in a language she
didn't understand. While the two men talked she
glanced through the doors and saw that the room was
an office. The walls were covered with charts and
maps, there were three fax machines, a row of tele-
phones and a computer unlike any she had ever seen.
Fran guessed that it was state of the art. So that was
where he did the deals that earned him a million a
day.

Ali noticed the direction of her glance and spoke
sharply to the man, who retreated into the office and
closed the door. Ali put his arm about Fran's shoulder,
guiding her firmly away. He was smiling, but there
was no mistaking the irresistible pressure he was ex-
erting.

'That is only my office,' he said. 'In there I do very
dull things that wouldn't interest you.'

'Who knows? Perhaps I would be interested?' Fran
said provocatively.

Ali laughed. 'Such a beautiful woman need think only how to be more beautiful still, and to please the man who is enchanted by her.'

How about that? Fran thought, annoyed. Prehistoric, male chauvinist—

Ali threw open another set of doors and Fran gasped at the sight that met her eyes. It was a large, luxuriously decorated room with a bay window, in which stood a table laid for two. The plates were the finest porcelain with heavy gold bands around the edge. By each place stood three glasses of priceless crystal. The cutlery was solid gold.

'It's beautiful,' she murmured.

'For you, nothing is too good,' Ali declared.

For me—or for whoever you happened to pick up, Fran thought, determined to keep her wits about her. But aloud all she said was, 'You're too kind.'

He led her to the table and pulled a chair out for her like the humblest of attendants. Part of the act, Fran decided, amused. All her journalistic instincts were on full alert, and while she seemed to be merely languidly accepting whatever happened she was actually observing every detail.

At the same time, she couldn't deny that she was enjoying herself. Ali was simply the most handsome man she'd ever seen. In the casino she'd seen him mainly sitting at the table, or at a distance. Now he was on his feet and close to her she felt the full impact of his magnificence.

He was about six feet two in height, with long legs and broad shoulders. Yet he didn't give the impression of being heavily built. He walked softly, making no sound, but nobody could have overlooked him. His movements had the lightness of a panther ready to spring.

His face was more than merely good-looking. It was a study in contradictions. At first glance it was European, inherited from his mother. Yet his Arab father was also there. Fran had read about Prince Saleem, a fierce man who inspired terror and devotion among his people. He too was in Ali's face in the dark chocolate eyes, the curved, stubborn mouth, and the air of proud authority.

Yet Ali had more than looks. His charisma was so strong that it was practically a force field. He radiated strength and intensity. And, while some of it must have come from having been born to rule, her instincts told her that his vibrant, emotional power was all his own.

He showed her to a seat, drawing the chair out and deferring to her. 'I will serve you myself, if that is agreeable to you?' he said smoothly.

'I am honoured to be attended by a prince,' Fran murmured.

She saw him smile, and guessed what he was thinking: this woman had fallen for his line, just like all the others. Well, if he thought that, he was in for a shock.

A heated trolley stood nearby, and he ladled a pale yellow liquid into a dish. It was thick, like porridge, mixed with rice, and it tasted delicious.

'Pumpkin soup,' Ali explained. 'I have a weakness for it, so when I'm here my chef keeps some permanently ready.' He served himself and sat facing her. The table was small, so even on opposite sides they were still close. 'Have you ever tasted Arabic food before?' he asked.

'A little. There's a restaurant I sometimes go to. It

has the most delicious chicken with dates and honey, and I can't resist it. But the surroundings are vulgar. The walls are covered with murals of the desert, with oases that light up in neon.'

Ali winced. 'I know the kind of place you mean. They make a great play of the desert, but none of them knows what the desert is really like.'

'What is it like?' Fran asked eagerly. 'Tell me about the desert.'

'How shall I know what to say? There are so many deserts. There is the desert in the evening when the sun turns to blood and is swallowed up by the sand. In England you have long twilights, but in my country it can be broad daylight, and then pitch darkness a few minutes later.

'Then, in the early hours, dawn lays a cool light on the land for a few moments, then rises in pale glory, and we all give thanks for the renewed blessing. But at noon the desert can be a enemy, and the sun turns to a furnace, driving you back into the sand.

'But they all have one thing in common, and that is the silence: a deeper silence than you can imagine. Until you have stood in the desert and watched the stars wheel overhead, you have never heard the silence of the earth as it spins on its axis.'

'Yes,' she whispered. 'That's what I thought.'

Without her knowing, a dreamy, far-away look had come into her eyes. Ali saw it, and a small frown of interest creased his brows. 'You thought?' he asked.

'I used to dream about places like that,' she admitted. 'When I was a child that dream was very important to me.'

'Tell me,' Ali said intently. 'What happened in your childhood?'

'It's strange, but whenever I think about that time I remember rain. I suppose it couldn't have rained every day, but all I can see is grey, drizzly skies, and people to match.'

'People were unkind to you?'

'No, I'm not being fair. After my parents died I was raised by some distant cousins on their farm. They meant well, but they were old and very serious, and knew nothing about children. They did their best for me, encouraged me to do well at school. But there was no excitement, and I longed for it.' She gave a small embarrassed laugh. 'You'll probably think this is silly, but I started to read *The Arabian Nights*.'

'I don't think that's silly. Why should I? I read it myself as a boy. I loved those fantastical tales, with their magic and drama.'

'There was certainly plenty of that,' Fran remembered. 'A sultan who took a new wife every night and killed her in the morning.'

'Until he found Scheherazade, who teased his mind with fantastic tales, so that he had to let her live to find out what came next,' Ali supplied. 'I loved the stories, but I loved Scheherazade's wit even more.

'I used to read that book in the desert, looking out at the horizon as the sun blazed its last before dying. How sad for you to yearn for the sun in this cold country.'

She nodded. 'Yes, and living in a chilly house, watching the rain outside, always short of pocket money because—I quote—"we mustn't be extravagant".'

She hadn't meant to make herself sound quite so deprived as it came out. Her elderly cousins hadn't been mean, simply determined to teach her the value of money. While rebelling at their frugal standards she'd somehow imbibed them. She'd gone on to achieve a first-class degree in economics, but pure economics had been too dry for her. So she'd switched to journalism, specialising in stories where scandal mingled with money. She'd found the excitement she secretly yearned for through investigating the shady secrets of high-profile figures. But she couldn't tell Ali Ben Saleem that.

There was a great deal more she couldn't tell him—like Uncle Dan's teachings about 'money and morality'. The God-fearing old man had never bought himself or his family any little treat without donating a similar amount to charity.

His wife had shared his views about thrifty living until Fran was sixteen and had suddenly blossomed into a beauty. Aunt Jean had yearned to celebrate the girl's looks with a new wardrobe, but it had taken many earnest discussions before Dan could be brought into the right frame of mind. The local charities had done well that summer.

They were both dead now, but their austere, kindly influence lingered. Fran had a passion for lovely clothes, but she never treated herself without also giving to a good cause. It was bred in the bone, and she wouldn't have known how to stop. It was hardly surprising that Sheikh Ali's lifestyle roused her to indignation.

'I know what you mean about restaurants that play up to stereotypes,' Ali said. 'I've been in places over here called Ye Old English Waterwheel, with waiters dressed as yeomen, tugging their forelocks, and saying, "What be thoy pleasure, maister?"' His stage yokel accent was so talented that Fran bubbled with laughter. He laughed with her and added, 'I nearly told them my pleasure would be to have them vanish from the face of the earth.'

'I suppose we both suffer from that kind of cliché about our countries,' Fran said.

'But England is also my country. I have an English mother, I attended Oxford University and learned soldiering at Sandhurst.'

She almost said, Yes, I know, but stopped herself in time. It wouldn't do to let him know she'd done her homework on him.

They had finished the pumpkin soup and Ali indicated a choice of dishes.

'If I had known your preference, I would have arranged for chicken with dates and honey,' he said. 'I promise it shall be served the next time we dine. Until then, perhaps you can find something in this humble selection.'

'This humble selection' stretched right down a long table. Fran was almost overwhelmed with choice. At last she picked a dish of long green beans.

'It's very hot,' he warned.

'The hotter the better,' she said recklessly.

But the first bite told her she'd made a mistake. The beans were spiced with onions, garlic, tomatoes and cayenne pepper.

'It's—it's delicious,' she said valiantly.

Ali grinned. 'You have steam coming out of your ears. Don't finish it if it's too much for you.'

'No, it's fine.' But she accepted some of the sliced tomatoes he pushed over to her, and to her relief they quenched the fire in her mouth.

'Try this instead,' Ali suggested, helping her to another dish. It was a cod liver salad and presented no problems. She began to relax even more. It was tempting to give herself up to the night's seductive spell.

And then, without warning, something disastrous happened. Glancing up, Fran met his eyes and found in them the last qualities she would have expected: real warmth, charm and—incredibly—a sense of fun. He was smiling at her, not seductively or cynically, but as though his mind danced in time with hers, and he was glad of it. And suddenly she suspected that this might be a truly delightful, great-hearted, funny, entrancing man. It was total disaster.

She struggled to clear her mind, but it persisted in lingering on the curve of his mouth, which was wide and flexible and made for kisses. It was smiling at her now in a special way that started a glow inside her.

And when she forced her attention away from his mouth his eyes were lying in wait to tease and entice her. There was a wicked promise in them and it was tempting to speculate what would happen to a woman who called that promise in. Of course, that could never be herself. She was here on serious business. But some lucky woman…

She pulled herself together.

'You have a lovely home,' she said, sounding slightly forced.

'Yes, it's beautiful,' he agreed. 'But I'm not sure it could be called a home. I have many dwellings, but I spend so little time in each one that—' He finished with a shrug.

'None of them is home?' Fran asked.

He gave a rueful smile. 'I feel like a small boy saying this, but wherever my mother is feels like my home. In her presence there is warmth and graciousness, and a sense of calm benevolence. You would like her very much.'

'I'm sure I should. She sounds like a great lady. Does she live in Kamar all the time?'

'Mostly. Sometimes she travels, but she doesn't care for flying. And—' he looked a little self-conscious '—she doesn't approve of some of my pleasures, so—'

'You mean like going to the casino?' Fran supplied, laughing.

'And other small indulgences,' he said outrageously. 'But mostly the casino. She says a man should have better things to do with his time.'

'She's right,' Fran said immediately.

'But how could I have spent this evening better than in meeting you?'

'You're not going to start telling me it was fate again, are you?'

'Have you suddenly become a cynic? What about all that Arabian folklore you used to enjoy? Didn't it teach you to believe in magic?'

'Well,' she said thoughtfully, 'it taught me to want to believe in magic, and that's almost the same thing. Sometimes, when life was very dull, I'd dream that a flying carpet was going to come through the window and carry me off to the land where genies came out of lamps and magicians cast their spells in clouds of coloured smoke.'

'And the magic prince?' he teased.

'He came out of the smoke, of course. But he always vanished in the smoke again, and the dream ended.'

'But you never stopped hoping for the flying carpet,' Ali said gently. 'You pretend to be very sensible and grown-up, but in your heart you're sure that one day it will come.'

She blushed a little. It was disconcerting to have him read her thoughts so well.

'I think that for you,' he said thoughtfully, 'the carpet will come.'

'I don't believe in magic,' she said, with a little shake of her head.

'But what do you call magic? When I saw you standing there tonight, that was magic far more potent than casting spells. And from that moment everything went well with me.' He gave her a wry smile. 'Do you know how much your witchcraft made me win? One hundred thousand. Look.'

Ali reached into his inside pocket, drew out a cheque book and calmly proceeded to write out a cheque for the full amount.

'What are you doing?' Fran gasped.

'I am giving you what is rightfully yours. You won this. Do with it as you will.'

He signed it with a flourish, then looked up at her, his eyes teasing. 'Who shall I make it out to? Come, admit defeat. Now you will have to tell me your name.'

'Oh, I don't think so,' she mused. She raised the glass, letting her eyes flirt with him over the rim. 'I'd be very foolish to give in right this minute, wouldn't I?'

'But I must have a name to put on the cheque.'

She shrugged.

'Without a name I can't give it to you.'

'Then keep it,' she said with an elegant gesture. 'I didn't ask you for anything.'

His eyes showed his admiration. 'You're not afraid to play for high stakes.'

'But I'm not playing for anything,' she said with a laugh. 'I've lived very happily without wealth and I can go on doing so.'

He cast a wry glance at her neck which wore a fortune in diamonds. Without hesitation Fran removed the necklace and set it beside him. 'Just so that there's no misunderstanding,' she said. 'I seek nothing from you. Nothing at all.'

It wasn't strictly true, but what she wanted from him would have to be told at another time, and another place. And then she would call the shots.

Their eyes held for a moment. His held bemusement that she should take their duel right up to the line. Finally there was a glimmer of respect.

With a shrug that mirrored the ones he'd given at the gaming tables, he pushed the cheque over to her, with the name still blank. Then he rose to his feet and made as if to fasten the necklace back in place. But Fran prevented him.

'You keep that. I'll keep this,' she said, indicating the cheque. 'After all, I don't want to be greedy, do I?'

Ali returned to his place opposite her and raised her hand to his lips, watching her all the time with eyes that were heavy, yet curiously alert. They were always alert, she realised, no matter what he was saying.

'Not many women can claim they've bested me,' he confessed. 'But I see you're used to playing games, and very good at it. I like that. It intrigues me. But what intrigues me even more is that smile you're giving me.'

'Smiles can convey so much more than words, don't you think?' she asked innocently.

'But what is conveyed without words can so easily be denied. Is that what you're doing, Diamond? Protecting yourself against the moment when you'll want to deny what is passing between us?'

It was like being naked, she thought, alarmed. He saw too much.

To divert his attention from the dangerous point she put the cheque in her purse. 'It would be very hard to deny that that has passed between us,' she observed.

'How true. I was sure a sharp wit lurked behind those innocent eyes.'

'You don't trust me, do you?' she asked impulsively.

'Not an inch. But we're equally matched, for I have the strangest feeling that you do not trust me.'

Fran's wide-eyed stare was a masterpiece of innocence. 'How could anyone doubt Your Highness's probity, rectitude, virtue, morality, righteousness—?'

He laughed until he almost choked, his eyes alight with real amusement, and he kissed her hand again, not seductively this time, but with a kind of vigorous triumph, as though he'd just seen his best hope romp past the winning post.

'What man could resist you?' he asked. 'Certainly I cannot. But stop calling me "Your highness". My name is Ali.'

'And mine is—Diamond.'

'I wonder. I begin to think I shall call you Scheherazade, for your wit, which is beyond the wit of all other women.'

'I'm cleverer than quite a few men too,' she riposted, and couldn't resist adding, 'You wait and see.'

He nodded. 'The waiting is half the pleasure. Will she say yes or no? And if she says no will her voice contain a secret invitation nonetheless?'

'I can't believe you ever have that problem. Don't tell me that any woman denies you.'

He shrugged. 'A man can have all the women in the world, yet not the one he wants. If that one denies him, what are all the others?'

Fran regarded him with wry amusement, not fooled by this. The words were humble but the tone was arrogant. Implicit was the fact that no woman refused him, but he felt it was polite to pretend otherwise.

'I'd have thought all the others were a good deal,' she said. 'They'd leave him no time for pining.'

'You speak like a woman who has never had her heart broken. I wonder if that can really be true?'

'It's true.'

'Then you have never loved, and that I find impossible to believe. You are made for love. I saw it in your eyes when they met mine in the casino.'

'You weren't thinking of love. You were thinking of money,' she said lightly.

'I was thinking of you and the spell you cast. It was that spell that turned my luck.'

'Oh, please! That's very pretty talk, but it was just chance.'

'For some there is no chance,' he said seriously. 'Whatever is written in the book of fate is what they put there themselves. I try to discern my fate through the smoke that surrounds it, and I see your handwriting.'

'And what—what else do you see?' she faltered.

'Nothing. The rest is hidden. There is only you.'

As he spoke he drew her to her feet and straight

into his arms. Fran had believed herself prepared for this moment, but when it came her well-laid plans seemed to fall away. His little teasing kisses in the car had carried the promise of what was to come, and now she knew that there was no way she could ever have left Ali tonight, without discovering if the promise would be kept.

It was kept magnificently. He enfolded her in his arms in a way that shut out the rest of the world, as though only she mattered. That alone was a seductive experience. Fran bestowed a brief thought on Howard—the man in her life as far as there was one. Howard was a banker, and he kissed like a banker, as though estimating profit and loss. Strange that she'd never thought of that before. Then Ali Ben Saleem's lips moved decisively over hers, and there were no thoughts left for any other man.

She told herself that she was merely laying the ground for the piece she would write, but her honesty wouldn't let her get away with that. This was the kind of experience a woman dreamed of, and it was irresistible.

His mouth was curved, strong, yet immensely subtle, and it knew what she wanted it to do before she knew it herself. He lightly caressed her mouth before brushing his lips over her eyes, her jaw, her neck. With unerring precision he found the little spot beneath her ear where she was unbearably sensitive and drew a soft, whispering line down the length of her neck. Nothing could have made her repress the sigh of pleasure she gave.

Her head was cradled on his arm while he searched her face, seeking there the answer to some question that was beyond words.

'Are you playing with me now?' he growled.

'Of course. A game that you don't understand.'

He liked that. 'When will I understand?'

'When it is ended.'

'When will it be ended?'

'When I have won.'

'Tell me your secret,' he demanded.

A smile touched her lips. 'You know the secret as well as I do.'

'With you, there would always be a new secret,' he said huskily, and covered her mouth again.

He half urged, half carried her the few steps to the couch by the window. She felt the cushions beneath her back and the moonlight on her face. He was caressing her with his lips while his hands began a gentle exploration of her body. She gasped at those soft touches. She hadn't known that she had such a body until his reverent fingertips told her, and told her also what it was for.

It was for giving and taking in an ecstasy of pleasure, and she hadn't suspected until this moment, when he made her understand what was possible beyond anything she could have imagined.

Her mouth moved feverishly against his, not receiving now but seeking and demanding with an urgency that astonished him—delighted him too, if his response was anything to go by. His insistence became fierce, and suddenly she could feel the hot breeze of the desert against her skin, see the dark red sun in its last moments before oblivion. He carried these things with him and no woman could lie in his arms without being aware of them as part of his soul.

All through the grey, chilly years this had been waiting for her, and now she had found it there was no turning back. He had said she was made for pleasure, and he was showing her that it was true.

She gave a long sigh, part acceptance, part apprehension. This was a very dangerous man. He could kiss, and kiss, until she no longer knew what was happening to her, or even who she was. And after that? Faintly, as if from a great distance, her pride was calling to her to save herself, because soon it would be too late…

But it was something else that saved her. A buzzer on the wall sounded faintly but persistently. Ali drew back with a small sound of annoyance, picked up a telephone nearby, and snapped something into it.

Almost at once his voice changed. Obviously the message was urgent, for he sighed and rose.

'Forgive me,' he said courteously. 'Important business calls me away.' He indicated the table. 'Please, pour yourself some wine. I shall be with you as soon as possible.'

He hurried from the room.

Still in a daze, Fran couldn't, at first, understand what had happened. At the height of a sensual experience such as she had never known before, he had simply brushed her aside. Business called and she had ceased to matter, or even to exist.

But when he returned he would expect her to be instantly available, she realised.

Well, now I know, she thought, seething. I came here to learn about Ali Ben Saleem, and I've already learned his priorities. Oil wells, one. Women, nil.

As her pulses slowed and she came out of the erotic dream he had induced with such infuriating ease, her anger grew.

'Who does he think I am?' she muttered.

No, not who? What? A doll to be put back on the shelf until he was ready to take her down again. And, as with a doll, he would expect to find her lying in the same position.

It would teach him a lesson not to find her at all.

She was on her feet in an instant, groping around for her sandals and trying to remember when and how she'd lost them. It brought home to her how far this man had lured her, how easily he'd made her lose control. She must escape.

She looked cautiously out into the hall.

A man, evidently a porter, sat by the front door. Fran wondered nervously if he had instructions to prevent her leaving. There was only one way to find out.

Taking a deep breath, she strolled across the marble floor, a picture of supreme confidence. The porter rose to his feet, uncertainty written all over his face. But, as Fran had hoped, none of his orders covered this unprecedented situation. Her heart thumping, she made an imperious gesture, and he bowed low as he opened the door for her to sail out into the night.

CHAPTER THREE

'YOU'RE crazy, going back into the lion's den,' Joey protested for the hundredth time.

'That's where it's most fun,' Fran said, putting the final touches to her immaculate appearance.

'You were lucky I was there to rescue you the other night.'

'Cut it out, Joey,' Fran chuckled. 'I walked out of his house under my own steam.'

'And found me waiting outside, in my car. I'd been on your tail ever since you left the casino.'

'But I won't need rescuing today. He's agreed to give me an interview.'

'Only he doesn't know it's you. And when he finds out he'll have a fit.'

Fran's eyes gleamed. 'That's what I'm looking forward to.'

She was almost unrecognisable as the siren of the other night. Instead of the seductive dress she wore a plain white silk blouse and grey business suit, with silver buttons.

Her glorious hair was smoothed back against her head. Her appearance radiated businesslike chic and quiet elegance. This was Ms Frances Callam, financial journalist. Diamond, the gorgeous creature who'd briefly scorched across the horizon, had been a mirage. Looking in the mirror, Fran could see no trace of her.

Which was almost a pity, she mused. Diamond had had a lot of fun. True, she'd also got herself into a perilous situation, from which she'd only just escaped. But she had escaped, and the whole event now looked like a thrilling adventure.

She gave a little sigh that was almost regretful. Suddenly her life seemed very lacking in adventure.

She disapproved of Sheikh Ali with every fibre of her being. She must keep reminding herself of that to dispel the sensual dream he'd woven around her, and which still lingered disturbingly.

At the time she'd fancied herself in control, but looking back she could see how disgracefully quickly she'd succumbed to a little cheap magic and a practised line.

But the scorching intensity of his lips on hers wouldn't be dismissed so easily. It haunted her night and day, filling her dreams so that she awoke wondering if she would ever know such sensations again. At work she tried to concentrate on figures, but they danced and turned into diamonds.

'I just hope the cheque clears before he sees you,' Joey said now.

With a start, Fran came out of her dream. 'I didn't take that money for myself,' she said. 'I made it out in favour of the International Children's Fund and handed it over to them yesterday. They'll be writing to thank him. I'd like to see his face when he gets that.'

Joey was pale. 'You gave away all that money?'

'Well, I couldn't have kept it,' she said, genuinely shocked.

'I sure would have done.'

Fran chuckled. 'I don't think he'd have given it to you.'

'I just can't believe he agreed to this interview.'

'I spoke to his secretary, and said that Frances Callam wanted to interview him for *The Financial Review*. I was given an appointment with no trouble.'

'Your taxi's here,' Joey said, looking out of the window. 'Sure you don't want me to drive you?'

'I think this time I should beard the lion completely alone.'

'I think I should be there waiting when he throws you out.'

'He isn't going to throw me out.'

'After the way you vanished and left him looking silly?'

'That merely told him that I can't be trifled with. Trust me, Joey. I'm right on top of it this time.'

Afterwards she was to remember the supreme self-confidence with which she got into the taxi and had herself taken back to the house of Ali Ben Saleem. It seemed so simple at the time.

At first nothing happened to change her mind. As soon as she rung the bell outside Ali's house the door was pulled open by the porter, who inclined his head in a silent question.

'Good morning,' Fran said. 'I have an appointment with Prince Ali Ben Saleem.'

She walked past him as she spoke, and into the centre of the tiled hallway. The porter hastened after her. He looked alarmed.

'Will you please inform His Highness that Frances Callam is here?'

At that moment the door to the office opened and Ali walked out. The porter made a sign of relief and backed towards the door. Fran took a deep breath and faced Ali, smiling.

He frowned when he saw her, then his face light-

ened and he advanced towards her, both hands out-
stretched, smiling in welcome.

Whatever she'd expected, it wasn't this. He should
have been annoyed at the memory of her desertion.
Perhaps he didn't recognise her. But his first words
dispelled that illusion.

'Diamond! My beautiful Diamond. What a pleasure
to see you again. Come.'

He gestured towards the dining room, and she followed him in.

'I know why you're here,' he said when he'd closed
the door behind them.

'You—you do?'

'You're angry with me about the other night. My
poor Diamond, it was so unchivalrous of me to leave
you and not return. My only excuse is that I was overwhelmed with business. I sent my secretary to make
sure you got home safely, but I would have liked to
see you myself.'

Fran took a deep breath, struggling for words while
various images flitted through her mind: kicking his
shins was the best, but boiling him in oil wasn't far
behind.

He hadn't come back at all.

All this time she'd been picturing his face when he
found her gone, and he didn't even know. He'd just
forgotten about her.

His secretary had probably been too afraid of his
wrath to admit that she wasn't there, and had invented
some story about having seen her home. The doorman,
too, had probably kept very quiet.

Then she saw Ali's eyes, glinting behind his smile,
and a doubt crept into her mind. Did he really not

know that she'd left? Or did he know, and had invented this story to turn the tables on her?

With this unpredictable man, anything was possible.

'I hope that some day soon we'll be able to enjoy the evening that was interrupted,' Ali continued, 'but just for the moment I'm afraid I'm very busy. In fact, you must leave at once, as I have an appointment with a journalist.'

'I thought you never saw journalists,' Fran said, getting ready to enjoy the next few minutes.

'Normally I don't, but Mr Callam is from a serious newspaper.'

'Did—did you say Mr Callam?'

'Mr Francis Callam. I've agreed to the interview because there are things it would suit me to make clear in his pages.'

Fran's thoughts were in a whirl. When they settled she gazed with delight on the resulting pattern. He was about to get the shock of his life.

'What kind of things?' she asked innocently.

Ali's smile was like a locked door. 'I wouldn't dream of boring you with such details.'

'Well, I know I'm just a stupid woman,' she said humbly, 'but I know how to spell financial. F-E—no, it's I, isn't it?'

He laughed. 'Your wit enchants me. Now, I've no more time for games. Mr Callam will be here at any moment.'

'Don't you want to know my name first?'

'I've already taken my own steps to discover it. I'll be in touch with you when I have time.'

'I wouldn't put you to so much trouble,' Fran said, breathing hard. 'My name is Frances Callam. Ms Frances Callam.'

She was fully revenged in the look that crossed his face. It was compounded of alarm, horror and anger.

'Are you telling me...?' he asked slowly.

'That I am the journalist you're waiting for. And I can not only spell financial, but I can add up. You know, one and one are two, two and two are four. I have a first-class economics degree, you see, and they insisted on it.'

His voice was very hard. 'You deceived me.'

'No, I didn't. I spoke to your secretary, and said Frances Callam wanted to talk to you for an article in *The Financial Review*. You both took it for granted it was a man because it never occurred to you that a financial journalist could be a woman. You fell into the trap of your own prejudice.'

'And the other night? Was it mere coincidence that you turned up at The Golden Chance?'

'No, I was observing you.'

'And afterwards? Do you dare say that wasn't deception?'

'We-ell, I may have left a few things out. But you made it easy.'

'And all the time you were laughing at me.' His eyes narrowed. 'Do you know what would happen, in my country, to a woman who dared to do that?'

'Tell me. No, wait!' She rummaged in her bag and produced a notebook. 'Now tell me. Hey!' Ali had firmly removed the notebook from her hand and tossed it aside.

'You will not make notes about me,' he said through gritted teeth. 'You will not write about anything that happened the other night—'

'Oh, I wasn't going to. I write for a serious paper.

It wouldn't be interested in that corny line you handed me.'

'I—'

'Well, you have to admit—burning sunsets and tents flapping in the breeze? But I don't blame you.'

'You don't?' He sounded dazed.

'I'm sure most girls would fall for it. Well, you wouldn't keep using it if they didn't, would you?'

'That's right,' he said, his eyes kindling. 'You see, one thing I've learned about women is this—the sillier the better.'

'You don't say!'

'The more foolish the line, the more unconvincing the stage props, the more chance that some fluffy-headed little girl is going to believe it. Experience has taught me all I need to know about your sex.'

'Are you daring to call me a fluffy-headed little girl?'

'I don't know why that should bother you, since you went out of your way to make me think just that. You should stick to the role, Miss Callam. It suits you better than pretending to be a man.'

'I'm doing no such thing,' she said furiously. 'I earn my living as a journalist. You promised me an interview, and I'm here. Why don't we get started?'

'If,' Ali said, regarding her coldly, 'you imagine for one moment that I intend to discuss my private affairs with you—'

'Not your private affairs, your business affairs,' Fran said. She couldn't resist adding provocatively, 'I think we've already covered the private ones.'

'Let it be clearly understood that I do not discuss business with women. That is not a woman's role.'

'Woman's role?' she echoed, scandalised. 'Why, you prehistoric—'

'Think what you like of me. Do you imagine I care? I haven't been used to considering the opinions of women and I see no reason to start now. In my country women know their place and keep to it. It's an arrangement that works very well.'

'I wonder what your mother thinks of that?' Fran said, with spirit. 'She's English, isn't she? Brought up to be equal with men—'

'No woman is equal with men. And don't speak about my mother. You're not going to interview me by the back door. I will not talk to you and that's final.'

'You talked all right when you thought I was just a plaything,' Frances snapped.

'But of course. That is what women are for.'

'It's not what I'm for.'

'You think so, but in my arms you came alive like a true woman. Don't say you've forgotten.'

She faced him defiantly. 'I was acting a part.'

He smiled, and something about it disturbed her obscurely. 'I don't think so. I can tell when a woman is pretending. I can also tell when she's yielding to her own deepest desires, in the arms of the man who can inflame those desires. Something happened between us the other night, something that was true and real.'

'As though anything true and real could happen between me and a man from the Stone Age.'

'Why must you deny it? What are you afraid of? That your theories might be swept away by a passion that will show you your real self? Is that why you try to reduce me to words on your page, because you think like that you will bring the truth under your control?'

He was standing dangerously close. She took a step away, and knew instantly that she'd made a tactical mistake. He knew now that she was nervous of him.

'The only truth I'm interested in where you're concerned,' she said, 'is what really goes on in those back-room deals you keep so secret.'

'And I tell you not to interfere in what doesn't concern you, and which would certainly be beyond your understanding. Please—' he held up a hand '—don't bore me with lectures about your brain. A woman's brain, for pity's sake!'

His scornful tone almost made her blow a gasket. 'We do have brains, you know! We are members of the same species. And you were ready enough to concede that Scheherazade had a brain the other night.'

'No. Scheherazade had wit. A woman's wit that sparkles and dazzles a man. Not a bludgeon to challenge him. I thought then that you were witty and subtle, but now you seem determined to prove me wrong.

'If you want me to listen to you, Diamond, forget your degree, and speak to me of your hair which is like a river of molten gold in the sunset. Then you will have all my attention. Since that night I've been troubled by your hair, thinking how I would run my hands through it and delight in adorning it with priceless jewels.

'I'm haunted, too, by your skin, which has the smoothness of satin. I've dreamed of how it would feel pressed against me when we lie together in bed—'

'Never,' she whispered in outrage.

He took a step closer to her and looked directly into her eyes. His own were burning.

'At this moment I too feel like saying never. I will never take to my bed a woman who rejects her own womanhood, and therefore my manhood. I will never trouble myself with a female who knows nothing about men and women and what fate created between them. I will throw her out and say good riddance.

'But then I look into the depths of your eyes, and I know that it isn't so easy. You and I met because we had to, and at our final parting we will neither of us be the same. What exquisite pleasure there will be in giving and taking with you, and knowing that what you give me you will have given no other man because you did not know it existed. That will be a treasure worth fighting for.'

He wasn't even touching her, but her heart was thumping wildly from the effect of his words and the images they conjured up in her fevered brain. She was fully clothed, but the caressing way he'd spoken of her skin had made it come alive. She felt as though his fingers were tracing soft paths across it, lingering, teasing her, and his tongue was driving her wild with flickering movements everywhere—her mouth, her breasts...making her want everything in the world, knowing that he was the one man who had it in his power to give.

She wanted to turn away, to refuse to meet his eyes and see in them the destiny he planned for her, whether she consented or not. But that would be cowardly. Danger must be faced, not avoided. And so she gazed on the picture he painted, and felt it swallow her up.

'Don't you feel that too?' he asked. 'That it must be so?'

'No,' she said, taking another step back from him.

'No, it can't be. You can't make something like that happen by giving an order.'

He reached for her. She backed but struck against the sofa, lost her balance, and had to sit on it. She tried to rise but he held her down with a hand on her shoulder, and sat beside her.

'But the order has already been given,' he said. 'And it was you who gave it. You came to The Golden Chance in search of me, and I recognised you at once as the woman who would play a special part in my life. It's too late to turn back. And why should you want to? Can it be that you are afraid?'

She would not let him kiss her, because he would take that as proof of his chauvinistic belief that only passion counted between men and women. And that was one victory he mustn't win. But while her resolve was strong her bones felt as if they had been turned to water.

Nor did he try to kiss her. He merely raised his hand and touched her lips softly with one fingertip, tracing the outline of her wide mouth. The sensations he could evoke by that simple gesture were shocking. She was on fire, and there was no hope for her.

She wanted to speak, to make an angry protest, but her mouth was quiveringly alive for the next gentle touch. Somehow—she didn't recall doing it—she'd taken hold of his arms, as if to steady herself, and the pressure of her fingers was drawing him close to her, until his lips were on hers.

As though this was a signal he'd waited for he took possession of the kiss, claiming her like a conqueror accepting surrender. Nor could she refuse because the treachery came from within herself, and it was her own desire that had invited him.

He had said that anticipation was half the pleasure, and he was a man who knew how to go slowly, prolonging his own pleasure and hers, teasing her with her own longings. She moaned softly, and he entered her mouth with quick, exploring movements that made her dizzy. She wanted to explore him in return, wanted it so much it alarmed her.

Before Ali, Fran had thought of herself as a moderate person. Howard's kisses had pleased her but never tormented her with the longing for more. Now she was discovering that her own propriety was nothing but a mask, behind which another woman—hot-blooded and demanding—was waiting to break forth into a new life. And it was happening with a man who drove her to a fury of antagonism, hand in hand with desire.

He gave her mouth a final caress, implicit with the promise of another time, and slid his lips down her neck, then further down, slipping open the buttons of her V-neck blouse to lay his lips between her breasts. The delight was unimaginable and her hands closed behind his head in a gesture of acceptance and plea. Her heart was thumping wildly beneath his lips, and she knew he must be able to feel it, but she was beyond caring. It felt as though everything about her was disintegrating and reforming into a new shape, a new person.

Then Ali raised his head and his eyes were hovering above her, reassured her that all was well as long as she was in his arms.

Slowly he lowered her back onto the cushions.

'You see?' he said, in a voice that shook a little.

'See?' she asked vaguely.

'When we are together—something happens—to you and to me—you can't deny it.'

'I don't,' she murmured. 'But it isn't—' She struggled to get the word out. 'Isn't important.'

'Passion is always important.'

Fran forced her head to clear. She didn't trust this man. And the more her body yearned for him, the more she distrusted him.

'But you feel passion for so many,' she managed to say.

He shook his head. 'Not—like that,' he said. And something in his voice told her that he was troubled. He'd done what he wanted, yet he too had been taken by surprise. He was shaking, and when he spoke again he sounded as though he was trying to force himself back to reality, because the realms of pleasure had alarmed him.

'Now you must go,' he said. 'For the moment. When the time is right for us to meet again, I will let you know.'

His arrogance had a usefully cooling effect on her. Angrily she freed herself and hastened to button up her blouse.

'You will let me know—when you have decided?'

'When the fates have decided,' he corrected her gently.

'Oh, no, you don't. I want the interview you promised me. If I leave without it, I won't come back, ever.'

'We'll see,' he said, smiling. 'But you will certainly leave without it.'

The world was resuming its normal shape. She changed tack. 'Now look, why don't you just be reasonable and we can—?'

'It's no use, Diamond. The answer is no.'

'And don't call me Diamond.'

'No, your name is Frances Callam. So, I needn't have gone to such lengths to find it out.'

'Didn't your secretary tell you? The one who saw me home?'

'It was no part of his duties to ask your name,' Ali said smoothly.

'But he must have told you where I lived,' she insisted. 'You could have discovered my name that way.'

His eyes flashed, and now she was certain that he had returned to find her gone, and this tale was an invention, so that she shouldn't know she'd successfully snubbed him.

'Why should I need such methods when I had a much better way?' he asked with a shrug. 'I have a small confession to make—about that cheque.'

'The one for a hundred thousand?'

'That's right.' He smiled straight into her eyes, and despite her annoyance Fran felt the return of disturbance deep within her, which had less to do with his sexual charisma than with his sheer charm. He shouldn't be allowed to smile like that.

'I'm afraid I stopped it,' Ali admitted. 'My bank will refuse to pay, but they will tell me who it's made out to. And so, if you hadn't come here today, I would have learned your name anyway.'

'Would you really?' she said slowly.

'Very unkind of me, wasn't it?'

'Very. But I did something rather unkind too. I didn't try to cash that cheque myself. I made it out to the International Children's Fund, and gave it to them yesterday, with your compliments.'

He laughed out loud, showing strong white teeth.

'That's very good, an excellent story. But, my dear Diamond, did you really think I'd believe that any woman could refuse such a sum of money?'

'I returned the necklace.'

'Worth about a tenth of the cheque. Giving away a hundred thousand would have been another matter.'

'Well, I did,' she said, getting cross. 'As you'll soon find out. When the cheque bounces, your name will be mud—probably in world headlines.'

'No, no, don't keep it up. It was a good try, but I'm not that easily fooled. Now I'm afraid you must go. You've caused me to waste too much time.'

'Yes, I mustn't disturb you from making money, must I?'

He saw her to the front door. 'Till our next meeting?'

'I wonder if there'll be one?'

'In my country we say—the answer is written in the sand.'

'And in my country we say—don't count your chickens before they're hatched.'

Ali watched her until she'd vanished from sight. As he turned back into the house his secretary was hurrying from the office, very pale.

'Excellency, someone from the ICF is on the phone to say they are most grateful for your generous cheque, but owing to a misunderstanding at the bank—'

Ali swore and vanished into the study. It took all his charm to smooth away the problem, and within five minutes a new cheque had been made out to the charity. As he sealed the envelope his eyes were unreadable.

'She fooled me,' he murmured. 'A hundred thousand, and nothing given in return.'

He took a sheet of paper and wrote on it 'Frances Callam'.

After regarding the name for a moment he crossed it out and wrote 'Diamond'.

Then he crossed that out, and wrote 'Scheherazade'.

CHAPTER FOUR

ALI BEN SALEEM'S house was quiet for a few days while he took a flying trip to New York. He returned in a hurry and spent the next week on the telephone, confirming deals and setting up new ones. Apart from his secretary, the staff saw very little of him, and he saw little of them. He certainly had no time to notice the new maid, which was what Fran had counted on.

It had been surprisingly easy to set up. Joey had mobilised his contacts to find an employment agency in the area. Using bribery and persuasion, he'd arranged for them to send out an advertisement to all the houses in the area, and Ali's chief steward had taken the bait. The house needed a live-in maid. Fran had applied, carefully disguised in a long, dark wig, drab clothes and flat shoes, and calling herself Jane. She'd been hired at once.

She'd thought long and hard before going under cover in Ali's house. It wasn't the way she liked to work, and she'd very nearly backed off.

But then the Sheikh had spoken in her mind: 'I do not discuss business with women... In my country women know their place and keep to it... No woman is equal with men.'

It was the memory of his imperious tone, as much as his words, that made her temper rise and her resolve harden. She knew she would have no peace until she'd made him unsay those words, and give her some respect.

51

She'd started on the day Ali departed. To begin with, her work had been downstairs, mostly in the kitchen. Once she was allowed upstairs, to clean Ali's bedroom, but only under the steward's supervision.

She'd found the room disappointingly austere. There was none of the silk-curtained luxury of downstairs, where Ali entertained ladies with names like Diamond. In his private domain Ali had plain white walls, polished floors and a large mahogany bed. Three pictures adorned the walls, all of them of horses. The steward had informed her that these were His Excellency's racehorses, shown at their moments of triumph in the Derby, the Grand National and at Ascot. Then he'd remembered his dignity, and told her sharply to get on with her work.

Fran wasn't sure exactly what she was looking for. Apart from getting a general picture of his life, she wanted something that would let him know she couldn't be simply dismissed, as he had done. It was proving hard to find.

She was working alone now. Joey had left London to take up another assignment in the north. She'd told Howard that she had to be out of town for a few weeks. Nobody knew where she was. She felt safer that way. But she was growing depressed by her lack of progress.

When Ali returned she kept well out of his sight, but it was hardly necessary. Sheikh Ali didn't notice servant girls.

But tonight it seemed he'd made a mistake. Watching from above, Fran had seen him go to his bedroom with files tucked under his arm. An hour later he'd been summoned downstairs by a late visitor, and gone down without locking his door.

This was her chance. Those files might contain some detail that would prove to be the key to the whole, involved oil empire. This man who spent a fortune on his pleasures and gave his people no say in the running of his little country must be made accountable. And she was the person to do it. If she also made him sorry he'd patronised her, that would merely be a bonus.

As soon as she saw him vanish she slipped down the stairs and into his room. The files were spread out on the bed. To her disappointment only one was in English, but she started on that.

She read rapidly, and as she did so her eyes widened with indignation. The documents concerned The Golden Choice, the casino where she and Ali had met, and they made it clear, beyond any misunderstanding, that Ali was the owner.

'The unscrupulous—' Words failed her, but she hurried to read as much as possible, her indignation growing.

Then, from behind her, came the ominous sound of a door being closed. Appalled, she looked up and found Ali standing there, regarding her with a cynically tolerant smile.

'I have to take my hat off to you,' he said. 'You don't give up, do you?'

Fran rose to her feet, trying to look dignified. It was difficult in the circumstances, but she did her best.

'You should have known I wouldn't give up,' she said defiantly.

'But I did know. The interest has been in seeing how far you were prepared to go. My dear Diamond—Frances—Jane—whatever you're calling yourself today—did you think I'd be so easily fooled?'

'You—knew it was me?'

'The advertisement that came through my door so conveniently, directing me to an employment agency? Of course I knew. I warned my steward to look out for you, and sure enough you turned up. To be fair, you did a good job. He barely recognised you. I knew you at once. There's something about you that no drab clothes can disguise.'

'You knew all along,' she repeated, in a daze.

'Poor Diamond. You thought you were doing so well.'

His smile never wavered as he spoke, but behind it lurked something that troubled her, something that would have frightened her if she'd been easily scared. Inside, he wasn't smiling. She was sure of it the next moment when he turned the key in the lock, and put it in his pocket.

'Hey, now, let me out of here,' she said, as firmly as she could.

'You want to rush away? Isn't that a little premature, seeing how much trouble you took to get in here?' He indicated the file she'd been reading. 'I do hope the result was worth it.'

That reminded her that she was aggrieved. 'You deceived me,' she said.

He began to laugh. 'I deceived you? You smuggled yourself into my house under false pretences, and I deceived you?'

'At the casino. It was a set-up. You own the place. No wonder you didn't mind losing. You were losing to yourself. And you fixed the winning too, making me think I was a lucky charm. Just another way of recycling the money to spend on enjoying yourself.'

'I didn't fix the winning,' he said. 'That would be

cheating, and beneath me. It just happened that way.'
He saw her sceptical look and snapped, 'I do not lie.'

'Of course not; I'm sorry.'

'You seem to have a very poor opinion of me. But
after everything that's happened I think we should de-
clare a draw and be friends.'

As he spoke he opened a mahogany cupboard, revealing a refrigerator within it. From it he took a bottle
of champagne, which he opened and poured into two
glasses.

'You won't refuse to drink champagne with me, will
you?' he asked. 'Or would you prefer a nice cup of
tea?'

'Tea would be very dull,' she said, recovering her
poise and accepting the glass.

She'd been surprised to find Ali taking this in good
part, but, after all, she hardly knew his character.
Doubtless he was feeling pleased at having wrong-
footed her, and the matter would end here.

'You're a most extraordinary woman, Diamond,' he
said affably, beginning to tidy away the files.

'My name is Fran,' she pointed out.

'I know, but I can't help thinking of you as
Diamond. Fran is such an abrupt name, but my
Diamond is the jewel who glittered for me that first
night, and has teased and tormented me ever since.
You must admit that after that cheque you owed me
the chance to get my revenge.'

Fran couldn't resist a smile. 'Yes,' she said. 'I read
in the paper about your generous donation. I really did
get the better of you, didn't I?'

She heard him give a swift intake of breath. He was
looking at her strangely, and for one moment she
thought she saw something in his eyes that he would

rather have concealed. Briefly it flashed in his eyes—
a look of cold menace, warning her to beware.

Then it was gone as completely as a desert mirage.
He was smiling as he said, 'No woman ever managed
that before.'

'I'm beginning to realise that I didn't know you at
all,' Fran admitted. 'I never dreamed that you'd be as
reasonable as this about it.'

'What did you expect?' he asked, amused.

'I'm not sure, but something outrageous and outside
the normal rules.'

'In other words, you thought I'd act like a stage
foreigner out of a cheap novelette,' he said, sounding
nettled. 'I'm a civilised man.'

'I know. It was very unfair of me.'

'So now that's settled I think we should toast each
other, as equal combatants.'

They chinked glasses.

'I wonder what you'll tell your confederates?' Ali
mused, sitting beside her on the bed.

'Luckily I have no confederates. I prefer to work
alone.'

'What about the little man who was with you at the
casino? Don't tell me you haven't been sending him
reports?'

'I only employ him occasionally. He's far away on
another job right now.'

'But your family—oh, no, you have none. What a
sad life!'

'It isn't sad at all.'

'But there's nobody to praise your successes, and
nobody to sympathise with your failures. It does seem
hard that you should have so little to show for your
efforts.' He looked at her thoughtfully, and seemed to

reach a sudden decision. 'All right! Perhaps I've been unreasonable. You may have your interview. There.'

'Do you mean that?' she asked eagerly.

'You can come and talk to me as soon as I return. That's a promise.'

'Return?'

'The man who just came to see me warned me of a crisis in Kamar that needs my immediate attention. I have to leave at once. But we'll talk when I get back.'

'When will that be?'

He shrugged. 'How can I tell?'

'Oh, I see,' she said in a deflated voice. 'That kind of promise. One day, never.'

'How suspicious you are! You think I mean never to return?'

'Well, if you do it'll be a long time, and you'll have forgotten we ever had this talk.'

'You may be right. In that case, you'll have to come with me.'

She gasped with delight. 'You mean that?'

'I'm a man of my word. You will be my guest in Kamar.' His eyes held a curious light. 'You will be privileged as no woman has ever been before, and I promise you an experience you will never forget.'

'When do we leave?'

'In half an hour.'

'But I don't have my passport.'

His ironic smile reminded her that he was a head of state. 'Leave me to worry about that. Hurry now! If you're not ready on time I'll depart without you.'

Fran didn't need any further encouragement. Filled with joy and relief, she bounded up and headed for the door. Laughing, Ali turned the key and let her out.

In her own room she threw her few clothes together and had just zipped up her bag when there was a knock on her door. Outside, she found a beautiful Arab girl, who bowed gracefully to her.

'I bring you these,' she said, holding out her arms which were filled with dark green robes. You wear— and you will be me.'

Through her fractured English she explained a little more, and Fran gathered that she was a Kamari servant in Ali's household, allowed to enter the country only to work for him. Fran would assume her identity, and her passport for both the outward and return journeys.

The girl helped her on with the robes, and showed her how to cover her head and swathe her face so that only the eyes were visible.

'But you must look down so that nobody sees your blue eyes,' she advised. 'Also, that is how a woman must walk, with eyes downcast. Not raise to master.'

Really, thought Fran ironically. It was a black mark against Ali, but she was feeling too much in charity with him to brood on it.

A few minutes later she was ready to join Ali's car, waiting at the front. He was already seated in the back, and she stared at the sight of him. He had discarded western clothes, and now looked every inch an Arab prince in splendid flowing white robes and headdress. He was absorbed in papers, but he looked up and indicated for her to sit beside him.

When she was settled the door slammed behind her, and the car began to move.

'You'll have to forgive me if I work,' he said. 'This crisis is going to take much of my attention.'

'What kind of crisis?' she ventured to ask.

'Don't ask me questions now.' A brief smile flitted

across his face. 'When we reach Kamar, all will be made clear to you.'

In half an hour they were at the airport. The car swung away from the main terminals towards the area where cargo planes and private aircraft operated. Looking out of the window, Fran saw the chauffeur get out and approach an official, handing him some documents which, she supposed, were the passports. The official glanced at the Rolls with its Kamari flag, proclaiming that the head of state was on board, and indicated for them to go through. It was easy if you were royalty.

The Rolls swung in a great arc and finally stopped. The chauffeur opened the door on Ali's side and bowed as his master got out. Fran followed and found herself standing before a private jet, painted in the blue and silver colours of Kamar. Ali was already headed up the steps without waiting to see if she followed, and she hurried to catch up with him.

The interior of the aircraft took her breath away. It was hung with silk curtains and the seats were large armchairs. A thick, multicoloured carpet covered the floor.

Ali seated himself alone, while someone waved Fran to a separate section of the plane. She guessed he'd retreated into loftiness because his employees were there, and for the moment she was prepared to play along with it.

The engines were already running, and as soon as the doors were closed the plane began to taxi. In another few minutes they were airborne.

Soon after take-off the steward fixed a small table in front of her, and served wine and almond biscuits. It was some time since she'd eaten, and she devoured them. Ali joined her for a few minutes, smiling at her excitement.

'I shall have to spend most of my time on the phone,' he said, 'but I have ordered that your needs should be attended to. There is a bed if you wish to sleep. It's gone midnight and this is quite a long flight.'

She yawned. 'I guess you're right. Perhaps a lie-down would be nice.'

He gestured with his head and the steward showed her the way to a separate compartment. Her jaw dropped as she saw the satin-draped double bed. This was more like a luxury hotel than an aircraft. But then, Sheikh Ali was like no other man.

She was almost ready for sleep, but she found that as soon as she lay down her yawns vanished. She was too excited to miss a moment, and she lay by the window, gazing through it at the lights on the wings, until the first gleam of dawn appeared on the far horizon.

She watched, transfixed, as the light grew until she could see the world, and she took a long breath of sheer wonder. Below her was sand as far as the eye could see. The sun was rising, and the desert lay in a pale half light, dim, mysterious. For the first time she realised its immense size. It was huge, featureless, and potentially as dangerous as the man who was taking her to it.

But danger was only a small part of the story. The fierce beauty of the desert struck some people like a fever from which they could never really be cured, and in that instant she knew that she was one of the afflicted. With joy she realised that she had come to the land of her dreams, the land that had haunted her ever since that lonely, rain-drenched childhood. And nothing in her life would ever be the same again.

She heard the door open, and the next minute Ali had dropped down beside her.

'There is my land,' he said. 'Waiting to welcome you.'

'It beautiful,' she said, awed. 'More beautiful than anything I could ever have imagined. It's so big and lonely—so—so self-sufficient.'

He looked at her with quick interest. 'You're right. That is what I have felt myself. The desert needs none of us. It is complete unto itself. How clever of you to understand that at once. Many people who are born here take a lifetime.'

She smiled, glad that he felt she was on his wavelength. It was a good start to her trip.

And then the sun finally appeared fully over the horizon, and the sand was flooded with smouldering light. Before her eyes it blossomed into deep yellow. The sky became a vivid, incredible blue, and the whole world seemed to glow.

'Thank you,' she murmured. 'Thank you for bringing me here.'

He shot her a troubled look that she didn't see.

'Come and sit down,' he said. 'We'll be landing any moment.'

She took her seat, still looking eagerly out of the window. Then the desert vanished, and they were coming in to land at Kamar's main airport, which looked exactly like every other airport. Another Rolls, with blacked-out windows, was waiting for them at the bottom of the steps.

Fran hastily adjusted her veil, lowered her eyes, and followed Ali demurely down the steps and into the back of the car. The door slammed, and they were moving.

The first part of the journey was uninteresting, along a long straight road that led from the airport to the city. Looking out of the darkened window, Fran saw the squat buildings of refineries.

But then they reached the city, full of early morning bustling, and at once her interest quickened. There was no time to see very much, for the car moved quickly, but she noticed that some of the people smiled and waved at the sight of the official flag. Whatever Ali was like as a ruler, his people were glad to have him among them again. Unless...

'Do they do that of their own free will?' she challenged Ali.

'Do what?'

'Wave and smile.'

She thought she heard him mutter, 'Give me patience!' Aloud he said sardonically, 'No, of course not. I issued a decree that anyone who doesn't look pleased to see me is beheaded in the market-place.'

'Sorry,' she said ruefully.

Ali glared, but relaxed into a sigh.

'I ought to have you beheaded for daring to insult me,' he said. 'But you'd only come back as a ghost and lecture me. Now be quiet and cover your face. We're nearly there.'

A few minutes later they swept beneath a huge archway and up to a broad flight of steps where several men in robes were waiting. One of them pulled open the car door.

'Remain here,' Ali commanded, and Fran stayed in her seat.

As he walked away someone else got into the car,

which moved off immediately. It was a tall woman, who removed her veil.

'I am Rasheeda,' she said. 'I am to take you to your apartments.'

She reached out and unhooked Fran's veil, fixing a long, hard look on her face. Her lips pursed critically, as though she disapproved of what she saw, and Fran began to feel that this was rather rude. But she concealed her indignation. With Ali's authority behind her, she had nothing to fear.

The car seemed to move for a long time, and she sensed that they were travelling right round to the back of the palace. Just before it came to a halt Rasheeda replaced her own veil, and nodded to Fran to do the same.

'Follow me,' she said as she left the car.

The way led up a flight of stairs, less ornate than at the front, and into a long, tiled corridor that was mercifully cool. In the few minutes between the car and the building Fran had felt the heat of the day that was rising fast. She breathed out, and Rasheeda gave her a quick glance.

'In your apartment you will find servants ready to make you comfortable,' she said.

'Thank you. You were expecting me, then?'

Rasheeda shrugged. 'We are always prepared for one more.'

It seemed a curious thing to say, but after puzzling it for a moment Fran shrugged. She would find her way around in time.

She had little time to look around, except to see that the building was exactly her idea of a traditional eastern palace. But the next moment they came to a lift.

Rasheeda pressed a button and soon they were flying upwards.

They walked along another corridor, until they stopped outside a door, bearing the number 37, which she pushed open. Inside Fran found a luxurious apartment, opening onto a balcony. An archway led to an ornate bathroom, covered in elaborate mosaics. Dazed, she realised that every fitting was solid gold. Rasheeda followed her gaze.

'You are much favoured,' she said briefly. 'I will summon your maidservants to prepare your bath now. You must be tired from your journey.'

'I don't seem to have my bag,' Fran said. 'Will it get here soon?'

'You will not be needing it.'

'But I will. All my things are in there.'

'Everything you could possibly need is here. His Highness prefers that his concubines accept only from his hands.'

'Excuse me? Did you say concubines? Look, there's been some mistake. I'm not a concubine. I'm a journalist.'

'I do not know what word you use in the west to describe such a woman as yourself.'

'But didn't Ali tell you——?'

'His Highness,' Rasheeda said, emphasising the words, 'telephoned me from the plane, giving me precise instructions for your reception. I am his mistress of concubines. I have followed my master's orders, and that is the end of the matter.'

'It certainly is not,' Fran said wrathfully. 'Are you saying that he dared to put me with his—his—?'

'It is a great honour for you,' Rasheeda said coldly. 'He will be most displeased at your ingratitude.'

'He's not the only one displeased,' Fran said. 'I'm going to see him now, and he's going to hear about my displeasure.'

She ran to the door and tried to pull it open, but it stayed firmly shut.

'Open this door at once,' she raged.

'His Highness's orders are that you remain here,' Rasheeda said firmly. 'Until he can find the time for you.'

'And just how long is that likely to be?'

'How can I tell? A week? A month? He has important things to attend to first.'

'Does he think he can get away with this?'

'His Highness is all-powerful and does as he pleases.'

Fran cast her a look of fury and ran past her, out onto the balcony.

'Help!' she cried. 'Help!'

She was four storeys up. Far below her stretched out a vast carpet of flowers and lawns. One or two men, presumably gardeners, glanced up at the sound of her voice, looked at each other, shrugged, and returned to their work.

Fran turned back into the room. The terrible truth was beginning to dawn on her. It was impossible, and yet, in her heart, she'd known that Ali was capable of anything, no matter how outrageous.

Rasheeda was standing beside the door.

'I shall leave you now,' she said, 'and send your attendants when you are more composed.'

She opened the door and quickly retreated. Fran made a desperate run, but she was too far away. By the time she reached the door it was already closed and locked. She hammered at it frantically.

'Let me out,' she cried. 'Let me out. You've got no right to do this!'

She listened, but there was only silence. She hammered again, harder this time.

'Let me out! *Let me out*!'

There was no response. She was left alone as the full horror of her situation dawned on her.

Ali had never meant to give her an interview. To him she was merely a woman who had dared to outwit him, and must be taught a lesson. He had tricked her into coming here, and now she was his prisoner, friendless, alone, with nobody to hear her cries.

In this country where he was all-powerful he might wreak what vengeance he pleased on her, and there was nothing she could do about it.

CHAPTER FIVE

WHEN she'd calmed down a little Fran began to explore her surroundings. Clearly there was no escape from the balcony, but she might find some other way.

She investigated her bathroom which, at any other time, would have delighted her with its luxury. The bath was sunk into the floor, and the smooth marble was delicious to the touch.

The main room was also opulent, with lavish hangings and a large bed, covered with rich crimson brocade and thick cushions. There were several doors, but they all led to closets. The only way out was by the main door, which was firmly locked. Fran groaned to think how stupidly she'd walked, wide-eyed, into what anyone could have seen was a trap.

And yet how could she possibly have anticipated such an outrageous action? In the modern world people just didn't do this kind of thing!

But Ali Ben Saleem wasn't a modern man. He was a sovereign ruler with absolute power, and he felt free to do exactly as he pleased.

She heard a key turn in the lock and looked up quickly, but it wasn't Ali. Two girls, dressed in the plain garb of maids, entered and inclined their heads respectfully towards her. One of them glided into the bathroom and began to run water into the sunken bath. Fran silenced her instinctive rebellion. She felt hot, sticky and tired, and the idea of a bath was suddenly very attractive.

The water was deliciously scented. Fran sank down into it and began to soap herself. Outwardly she was acquiescent. Inwardly she was planning just what she would say to Ali when she saw him. But when would that be? Rasheeda had hinted that she might be left here for a long time before that happened.

When she was ready to climb out of the bath the two maids held up a white towel to wrap around her. She finished drying and looked around for her clothes. There was no sign of the plain green tunic she had worn to enter the country.

Instead, one of the maids made a smiling gesture to some elaborate robes in peacock-blue that were hung up ready for her.

'I'd rather wear my own clothes,' Fran said firmly. 'They're in my bag. Where is it, please?'

One of the maids frowned. 'Bag is missing,' she said. 'These are your clothes.'

'Oh, no, they're not. If your master thinks he's going to dress me as one of his fancy women, he can think again!'

'Please,' the maid begged, 'do not speak disrespectfully of master.'

'I'll say a few disrespectful things to his face when I see him. I want my bag.'

They stared at her blankly.

Against all reason Fran dug her heels in. 'I'll wear my own clothes or nothing,' she said firmly.

Turning her back on them, she sat down on one of the heavily cushioned sofas, pulling the towel around her, and wishing it were larger.

Behind her she could hear whispering, as though the maids were conferring together about how best to cope with her rebellion.

'I am not giving in about this,' she said, as decisively as she could manage.

'That's my Diamond,' said an amused voice.

Fran leapt up and whirled around. Ali stood there, arms akimbo, regarding her sardonically. The maids had vanished.

'You!' she said angrily. 'How dare you?'

Ali grinned. 'How dare I what?'

How dared he stand there looking so handsome, and so assured? That was the thought that scorched across her brain before she could stop it, but she quickly substituted, How dared he behave so disgracefully?

'If this is your idea of a joke, then it's misfired badly,' she said with dignity.

'Tell me.' He folded his arms and regarded her.

'I'm here to write a story—the one you promised me. You thought it would be very funny to dump me in this place and lock the door. All right. It was funny. But now it's ''joke over'' time and I want to start getting serious.'

He looked her up and down, taking in the towel and the bits of her that it left uncovered. It reached only just to the top of her thighs. At the upper edge it was twisted into a makeshift knot just above her breasts, but with every breath she took Fran could feel it threatening to come loose. She put a protective hand over the knot, wishing Ali would stop looking at her in a way that showed he understood the danger as well as she did.

'But I am serious,' he said at last. 'Diamond, for a woman who prides herself on having a brain, you are easily deluded. I told you once there would be no interview and no story. I haven't budged from that position, and you were naive to imagine that I would.'

She heard the words but could hardly take in their meaning. It was simply too monstrous. 'You—never meant to talk to me?' she breathed.

'Not for a moment. Money, business, politics—these things are not the concern of women. I told you that, but you wouldn't believe me.'

'You lured me here on false pretences. You had no right—'

'But you should have guessed that I'd do something like this. You knew I was the kind of man who would never forgive an injury.' He took a step closer, looking down at her. For a moment there was a hint of menace in his soft voice. 'How foolish of you to forget that.'

'What injury? I've never harmed you.'

'You forced my hand over the cheque. That stung my pride.'

'Your pride!' she scoffed.

His voice changed, became harder. 'The ruler of a country must be a man of pride. If not, he is unfit to rule. I could not allow an insult to go unpunished. You invaded my home in disguise—two disguises if you include the night we met. You thought you were very clever, but you weren't as clever as you imagined. I decided it was time you had a lesson in reality.'

'Reality?' she echoed, hardly able to believe her ears. 'You call this reality? Putting me with your concubines?'

'You have only yourself to blame. You challenged me, and I took up your challenge. The next move is yours.'

'Yes, and it will be, when people start asking questions about my disappearance.'

'But when will that be? You told me yourself, nobody knows you came to work under cover in my house. Your friend Joey is away on another job. You have no family. Who will know that you are gone?'

'And bringing me here on someone else's passport...?' she whispered.

Ali nodded. 'Nobody will know that you have left the country, much less where you are.'

With mounting anger she realised the full horror of her situation.

'All those questions you asked me last night about how I was going to tell my confederates?—you were checking whether it was safe to kidnap me. You were planning this then.'

'I'm a man of foresight.'

She made one last attempt.

'Ali, this has gone far enough. I want my bag, my clothes, and I want to get out of here.'

He laughed softly. 'Oh, my Diamond, you are wonderful. You have no weapons, you are completely helpless in my power. Yet you speak with such authority, as though you had only to command and I must obey. I tremble in my shoes.'

'I don't believe this,' she said in a shaking voice. 'I'm dreaming, and I'll wake up soon.'

'I wish you the sweetest of dreams, and I hope they will all be of me. But when you awake you will still be here. And you will remain here, at my pleasure, until I decide otherwise.'

'You're utterly mad,' she breathed. 'You must be, to imagine that you can turn me into a concubine—number 37!'

He laughed. 'Well, I have to admit that I don't actually have thirty-seven. This is simply the only room with a lock on the door. The others don't have to be locked in. They enjoy serving their country.'

'Well, this isn't my country, and I have no intention of serving it in your bed,' Fran said emphatically. 'If the others are so keen, why not stick to them?'

'If you knew how often I've asked myself the same question. But you tease and provoke me as they do not.'

As he spoke he placed the back of one finger on her shoulder, and trailed it down the length of her arm. The touch was light, almost imperceptible, but it was enough to send tremors through her whole body. When he removed his hand she could still feel the tingling all down her arm.

She took a deep breath, trying to stop herself from shaking. It dismayed her to discover that her physical response to Ali was as intense as ever, even now when she was furiously angry with him. Of course he'd counted on that. He expected her to collapse before his male potency, and if it was the last thing she did she would prove him wrong. She lifted her head and met his eyes defiantly.

'I demand that you release me,' she said.

'Magnificent,' Ali murmured. 'At this moment I admire you more than ever.'

'Did you hear what I said?'

'Of course I heard, as I hear the splash of rain on the windows. I hear the sound, but it doesn't stop me in my course.' He lifted her chin. 'Be patient, Diamond. Did I not tell you that the pleasure lies in the anticipation? And we have much to look forward to. When the moment comes, we will be as no man and woman have ever been before.'

It was hard to deny it when his fingertips were stroking her mouth, but she forced herself.

'That will never happen,' she said. 'I refuse. If you

think that this—' she made a sweeping gesture around the room '—and all your power makes any difference, you're fooling yourself.'

He laughed softly. 'I think you'll find that it does make a difference. But fight me if you like. It will only make my eventual victory the sweeter.' He sighed ruefully. 'Let's hope that affairs of state don't detain me too long, and I can find time for you soon.'

She stared as his incredible meaning sank in. Then something in her snapped.

'No!' she screamed. *'No!'*

Evading his grasp, she darted to the door and began to hammer on it. 'Somebody—help!'

In a flash he was with her, putting both arms around her and lifting her off the floor to carry her into the middle of the room. She thrashed and kicked but his grasp was unbreakable, and all she achieved was to loosen the towel, which began to slip away from her.

'Let me go!' she screamed. *'Let me—'*

The sound was cut off by his mouth over hers, in the most ruthless kiss he had ever given her. It was not a caress but an assertion of dominance, silencing her completely. She put out all her strength to resist him. She would not let herself be kissed like this.

But he kissed her anyway, as never before. Their other kisses had been like fencing matches, with the power evenly balanced. This time he was determined to overcome her. The towel fell, unnoticed, to the floor, and he was holding her naked body in his arms, while his lips told her silently that she belonged to him, whatever she might say.

When he felt her still trying to struggle he murmured, 'Don't be foolish, my Diamond. You could overcome me more easily than you know, but not by force. You have weapons that could enslave a man.'

He turned her in his arms, putting a hand under her knees and raising her to carry her to the bed. Without removing his mouth from hers he lowered her onto the satin cushions. She clung to him, perhaps to steady herself, perhaps because she couldn't do anything else.

She became aware that his embrace had changed. The fierceness had gone out of it, leaving behind only tenderness, and coaxing. Something deep in her took fright at that coaxing. It contained a greater power than any threat. His lips were seductive, teasing her into compliance, persuading her that there was nothing she wanted to do but this.

He left her mouth and began to kiss her down the length of her neck, then down further to the place between her breasts. He lingered a moment, and Fran knew he must be able to feel the hammering of her heart.

'Does your heart beat with love or hate, Diamond?' he whispered.

'With hate,' she managed to say.

'And mine?' He took her hand and placed it over his own heart, which was beating as strongly as her own. 'What of mine? Is that love or hate you feel there?'

'Neither,' she gasped. 'All you want is possession.'

'Perhaps. There has never been a woman I wanted to possess as much as you, or for whom I would take such risks. Ask whatever you will of me.'

'Let me go,' she said fiercely.

The words stopped him in his tracks. He released her and drew back, his face a cold mask.

'You ask the impossible,' he grated. 'It's time you faced the truth. You'll stay here until I'm satisfied.'

'And when will that be?'

A strange, distant look came into his eyes, as though he was communicating with a vision only he could see.

'When you yield to me completely, in your heart as well as your body. When you say that you are mine for all time and desire only to remain with me. Then, and only then, will I be satisfied.'

Moving quickly, he rose and backed away.

'But I won't stay here,' she raged. 'I'll escape and expose you to the world.'

She was talking to a closed door.

Fran was too intelligent to keep fighting the same battle with the same discredited weapons. So she calmed her temper and assumed an attitude of compliance, to hide her inner rebellion and her determination to escape.

She realised she was exhausted. She hadn't slept the night before. Now she was determined to keep up her strength, so she slipped between the sheets of the lavish bed, and slept the sleep of the jet-lagged.

When she awoke her maids were present, bowing and smiling, and indicating a meal that was ready for her. It was a meal for an honoured guest—veal and apricots, followed by stuffed dates and wine. It was delicious and she realised that she was very hungry.

While she'd slept her bag had been returned to her. Diving into it, she discovered that something was missing. Her notebooks and Dictaphone machine were there, but not her mobile phone.

So, no chance to call for help.

The maid who understood some English, and whose name was Leena, explained that the rest of the afternoon would be taken up by a visit from a maker of materials, who would produce samples for her choice.

'Then make—to your liking,' she said.

Fran would have liked to say that she wasn't going to be here long enough to make a new wardrobe necessary, but she merely nodded and smiled. An appearance of agreement was simply part of the role she was playing for the moment.

But her pose was shaken when the merchant appeared and tossed bolt after bolt of fabric at her feet, until the floor was covered with a myriad colours.

'Where do I start?' she gasped.

'My master says—everything you wish,' Leena said, smiling.

Fran pulled herself together. She absolutely would not let herself weaken because of a few bolts of silk, even if one of them was guaranteed to highlight her eyes, and another would bring a peachy glow to her skin.

Since it was clearly expected of her she ran her hands over the material, feeling the luxurious sensation against her skin. It was her undoing. Suddenly she was a teenager again, pressing her nose against the shop window, yearning for the clothes within. Only this time someone had removed the window, and the clothes were hers.

A subtle intelligence had been at work here. Somebody understood what would make her weaken—if anything could. She would select only the bare minimum.

Two hours later the merchant departed jubilantly,

with the largest order he'd ever been given, even from the palace.

Fran was left aghast, wondering what had come over her. It wasn't just the material, but the fortune in jewels that Leena had calmly ordered to be sewn into the garments. When Fran had asked if these were real jewels Leena had been shocked. As though the Prince of Kamar would give anything less!

'But of course these are only little jewels,' she had explained. 'The master will present you with the big ones himself.'

'The—big ones?' Fran had said, dazed.

'You are to be greatly honoured. He has said so.'

Honoured with everything but my freedom, Fran thought.

But she held her tongue. When she next saw Ali she would have plenty to say.

It was early evening. Fran went out onto the balcony and watched the last few minutes of daylight before the light vanished and it was pitch-dark, almost as though somebody had thrown a switch.

Even in her present mood she had to admit that this was a magic place at night. Below her were the palace gardens, hung with a thousand coloured lamps, glowing against the velvety blackness. Beyond that was the city, with its own lights, hinting at a rich, busy life. From somewhere below the sound of music floated up to her.

Looking down, she could see the paths that crisscrossed in the garden, and the figures that strolled in the blessed cool of the evening. One of them might almost have been Ali.

She peered at the tall figure in the white robes and gold agal. She couldn't see his face, but his bearing and the way he moved made her sure that it was Ali. He was talking to someone by his side, someone smaller, whose head was covered and who might have been a woman...

Fran didn't even realise that she'd tensed, leaning forward a little more, and a little more, until the figure turned—and she saw his beard. Then she discovered that she was gripping the rail with all her strength. She released it, feeling the waves of relief wash through her so fiercely that she felt faint.

To make it worse, Ali looked up at that moment. She stepped away so that he shouldn't catch her looking at him. But she was sure he would have seen her. She turned quickly back into the room.

To pass the time she pulled out some of the books she found on a shelf near her bed. They were in English, and all about Kamar.

She had already learned a good deal about the country in her preparation for the feature, but this book concentrated more on the men who had shaped the principality.

Kamar was barely sixty years old. It had become a self-governing state because one determined man, Najeeb, had appeared out of the desert, sat himself and his tribe down on the first oil well, and refused to budge. He was the man the oil companies had had to deal with, and when he'd declared himself sovereign it had been easier not to argue.

He didn't sound a very pleasant man, Fran thought, but he'd had vision, courage, determination and obstinacy. He'd been Ali's grandfather.

His son, Najeeb the second, had made money easily and spent it easily. He'd had two sons, who had quarrelled for the throne, and the younger, Saleem, had triumphed. Saleem had opened up Kamar to modern technology, and seemed to have been an enlightened ruler.

The photographs showed men with curiously similar faces, fierce, hard, seeming to look out on far desert horizons. They all had a noticeable unyielding quality about the mouth and chin, the same quality Fran had seen in Ali's face. He came from a line of men who were ruthless by nature, and also because ruthlessness was the only thing that paid. And he was one of them.

She was suddenly unwilling to read any more. She closed the book sharply. At once Leena was on her feet, urging that it was time to retire. Fran agreed.

It seemed that Leena would stay with her, sleeping on a small truckle bed, in case she should want anything during the night. Fran's attempts to shoo her away proved fruitless, so she resigned herself. And when she awoke in the early hours, with a parched throat, it was pleasant to have someone make her some herbal tea that sent her back to a dreamless sleep.

CHAPTER SIX

IN THE morning Leena had a surprise for her.

'We can go to the bazaar and do some shopping, if it is your wish,' she suggested.

So she wasn't to be kept locked in the palace all the time, Fran reflected. Perhaps while she was out she would find a chance to contact the British ambassador.

The maids dressed her in the peacock robes, and set the matching turban on her head. The veil was connected to one side of this, and could be drawn across her face to be hooked onto the other side.

Outside the door she found four large men waiting, their arms folded.

'They are your guard of honour,' Leena explained.

'Oh, I see,' Fran said wryly.

A stretch limousine waited below. One of the guards drove, the other three settled into the first compartment. Fran and Leena went into the second compartment. The car began to draw away.

But before they had travelled a couple of yards there was the sound of footsteps outside and one of the doors to the rear compartment was wrenched open. Next moment, a man had settled himself on the seat facing Fran, and pulled the door shut.

'Get out!' shrieked Leena. Then her hands flew to her mouth and she whispered, 'My lord!'

It wasn't Ali but a young man who resembled him, except that his expression was lighter and his eyes twinkled with merriment.

'I couldn't resist having a look at my cousin's latest acquisition,' he said cheerfully.

'Your veil,' Leena gasped to Fran.

'Too late, I've seen her face now,' the young man said. He smiled at Fran. 'I am Prince Yasir, Ali's cousin. Tell me, are the stories true? Did Ali really pay a hundred thousand for you?'

'*Pay?*' Fran gasped.

'That's what the rumours say. Most women don't come so expensive. I've never paid more than thirty thousand myself, but Ali acquires only the best, and I can see you're something out of the ordinary.'

'Get out of here at once!' Fran exploded. 'Go on! Get out before I kick you out.'

Leena shrieked, but the young man merely roared with laughter. 'And with the spirit of the devil. You were worth every penny. Goodbye—until we meet again.'

The next moment he opened the door and jumped out while the car was still moving.

'He is a prince,' Leena moaned, 'and you threatened him. The royal displeasure will fall on us.'

'Nonsense!' Fran said robustly. 'How dare he suggest that I was bought?'

'But everyone says you cost Prince Ali a hundred thousand,' Leena protested.

'He gave that much to charity because—that is—to please me,' Fran said, choosing her words carefully.

Leena gasped. 'Then he must value you greatly.'

So now she knew how she was regarded here, Fran thought: as a high-priced acquisition, on a level with a jewel or a racehorse. No doubt Ali saw her in the same light.

Then she forgot her indignation in her excitement

at being in the bazaar. As the limousine glided through the streets people backed away and bowed to the royal flag, although the darkened windows meant that they couldn't see inside. They drew to a halt. Leena settled Fran's veil back in place, and they stepped out of the car.

She gasped as she felt the noonday sun beating down on her. But when she'd had a few minutes to accustom herself she enjoyed the heat, the brilliant light and the dazzling colours. If this had been a holiday she would have revelled in it. As it was, the guard of honour constantly reminded her that she was a prisoner, although an honoured one.

Since she could order anything she wanted at the palace, there was little for her to buy in the street, but she chose a pair of white doves, whose cooing and friendly ways enchanted her. The vendor assured her, through Leena, that no cage was necessary.

'Win their love, and they will stay with you,' he promised.

'He means they will fly back to him and he can sell them again,' Leena said indignantly. 'We'll have a cage.'

'No,' Fran said. 'No cage.'

Leena started to argue, but Fran silenced her. She took a bag of food from the vendor, and used it to entice the doves into the car. As they got in, Fran could see the driver talking into the car phone. She discovered why when she reached her room to find a dovecote already set up on the balcony.

To her delight the doves seemed pleased with their new home, and showed no inclination to fly away.

'Not like me,' she murmured to them. 'I'll fly at the first opportunity.'

There was a light snack, then Leena seemed mysteriously anxious for Fran to take a nap. But she refused to say why this was so important, until Fran had awoken and was taking a cooling bath.

'What's that?' she demanded as Leena poured a sweet-smelling lotion into the water. Eyes closed, she breathed it in, and instantly strange thoughts began to float through her mind. It was a heady, erotic scent, hinting of passion incited and fulfilled. It was a perfume for lovers, and she breathed it in with relish.

Then abruptly she opened her eyes, assailed by suspicion. 'I'm getting out of here,' she said firmly, and climbed out of the tub. 'And when I've had supper I'm going to bed for a very early night.'

'But I have to prepare you for the master. He has chosen you to be his companion tonight. You are most honoured among women.'

'Fiddlesticks!' Fran said shortly. 'If you think I'm going to let you do me up like a turkey being prepared for the table, you're very much mistaken.'

'But it is the custom,' Leena wailed. 'To be chosen by the great lord is the finest thing that can happen to a concubine.'

'I'm not a concubine!'

'The chosen one is bowed down with honour.'

'Not this chosen one!' Fran snapped. 'I'm not going to be bowed down with anything. I shall go with my head up, look him in the eye and tell him what I think of him.'

'But properly attired,' Leena begged. 'Or I am in trouble.'

'Very well. Only for your sake.'

The seamstresses had worked through the night and the first of Fran's new clothes was ready. It was a marvel in pale fawn satin and brocade, with a wide, jewel-encrusted sash around the tiny waist. Over it was a tunic of diaphanous silk gauze, also glittering with jewels. When the matching turban was in place Fran drew a disbelieving breath at the sight of the Arab beauty who looked back at her from the mirror.

Ali seemed to be there with her, whispering 'I told you so', his eyes glowing with desire...

She drew a sharp breath and castigated herself. She was furious with Ali, set on leaving him at the first chance and never seeing him again. She must remember that.

The door opened and Rasheeda entered. It was the first time Fran had seen the mistress of concubines since the first day. Rasheeda regarded her loftily, then nodded her approval. Leena visibly relaxed.

From outside the door came the melancholy, mysterious sound of a horn being blown.

'Your litter is here,' Rasheeda said, adjusting Fran's veil. 'You will travel inside it to His Highness's apartments, and I will walk ahead proclaiming your coming. When you see the prince, remember to bow low and say, "Your humble servant greets you, my lord." Do not meet his eyes unless he tells you to. To look at him without his permission is a grave offence. Do you understand?'

'I understand,' Fran said, breathing hard.

Rasheeda opened the door, four large men carried a curtained litter inside, and set it down. Leena parted the curtains for Fran to step in, closed the curtains firmly again, and they were on their way.

The litter was carried by men chosen for their size and strength. The inside was fitted with gold, inlaid with rubies and emeralds, and furnished with gold satin. The sides were shielded by curtains of white and gold brocade.

The journey seemed to take for ever. Shut away behind the curtains, Fran could only guess what was happening. In front of her she could hear the sound of the horn, followed by Rasheeda crying out words in Arabic.

She spent the time trying to sort out her thoughts and prepare what she was going to say to Ali. It would be like him, she thought crossly, not to be there when she arrived.

But he was there. She heard him speaking to the bearers, then the sound of feet retreating, the door closing.

'You can get out now,' came Ali's amused voice.

Fran leapt out of the litter and looked around for him, but Ali had retreated to a safe distance and was watching her with laughing eyes. Fran snatched away her veil and faced him.

'If you have the nerve to think that "your humble servant" is going to bow to you—'

'But I don't,' he said, laughing. 'That's why I took the precaution of making sure we were alone first. If my servants had seen you greet me disrespectfully I should have had to cast you into a snakepit, which would rather have spoiled our evening.'

Fran regarded him. 'How dare you send for me as though you had only to snap your fingers and I must jump to attention?' she seethed.

'But I'm afraid that's exactly true,' Ali said apologetically. 'I appreciate that you are unfamiliar with this arrangement, but don't worry. You'll get used to it.'

'Not in a million years!'

'Will you and I be provoking each other for a mil-

lion years, my Diamond? What a wonderful prospect.'
His eyes smiled at her, in a way that almost made her
forget her anger. 'How beautiful you are!'

'Don't try to change the subject.'

'To me, your beauty is always the subject. How
your eyes enthral me!' He deftly removed the turban,
letting her hair fall freely about her shoulders, and
running his hands through it. 'And your hair! How I
have dreamed of your hair!' He drew her into his arms.
'And of your lips,' he said, covering them.

A thousand answers jostled in her brain, but with
her mouth engaged with his possessive kisses she
could make none of them. She tried to hold onto rational thought, but she was just realising that she had
secretly longed for his embrace. Throughout all her
justified indignation, that yearning had been there, like
a subtle, endlessly repeated chord. Now she had what
her flesh wanted and her mind resisted.

'Tell me,' he whispered, 'haven't you dreamed of
me, just a little?'

'Yes,' she said, and watched the eager light come
into his eyes. 'I've dreamed of how I was going to
make you very, very sorry. I enjoyed those dreams.'

'How hard-hearted you are!' he chided her softly.

'*I'm—?*'

Whatever else she was going to say was cut off by
his mouth on hers. She should have been ready for
him, but nothing could have prepared her for the
scorching intensity with which he caressed her lips
again and again, until she gasped from the sensation.

'Such a battle we will have,' he whispered. 'And
how we will enjoy the victory!'

'Whose victory?'

'When we lie in each other's arms it will be a victory for both of us. Otherwise it will not be a true loving. We must look to the night ahead with joy.'

'We—'

'But for a while we must wait,' he added, releasing her. 'Passion, like many things, must be deferred so that it's full savour can be appreciated. Try to be a little patient.'

Fran was speechless. To give herself the relief of exercise she began to pace Ali's apartment, which was stupendous in its luxury. It was a kind of labyrinth, with horseshoe arches leading off in all directions. The mosaics on the walls were inlaid with intricately worked gold that gleamed richly in the soft light.

They were in a large room with several tables, laden with every possible variety of food. Instead of chairs, long couches were strewn around, as though for an orgy. But there were just the two of them.

'It's shocking, isn't it?' Ali said, reading her face.

'Yes, it is,' she responded indignantly. 'Nobody has the right to live like this when there are people starving.' She studied one of the walls and added, 'It looks new.'

'You sound as though that made it worse.'

'It does. If this was an old palace I might—'

'Forgive me?'

'Understand the need. I mean, if it's there anyway—but building from scratch—all that money—'

'Blame my great-grandfather, Najeeb. He built the first palace, but it wasn't big enough, so his son had to build this one.'

'The first palace?'

'I love you when your eyes pop with virtuous indignation. Come out onto the balcony and I'll show you the Sahar Palace. It's called that because Sahar means dawn, and with its high tower it catches the dawn sun before any other building.'

His balcony looked out over the city. Following his pointing finger, she just made out Sahar Palace. It was hard because the building was in darkness. Simply abandoned, she thought crossly. Her fingers itched to get at her Dictaphone and make notes of the waste and extravagance in this country. Luckily her memory was excellent.

'Can you put your puritan scruples aside long enough to eat something?' Ali asked, taking her hand and leading her to where a banquet was laid out on long tables decked with flowers.

'I hope the food is to your liking,' he said, pointing to one dish.

'Chicken with dates and honey,' Fran said in wonder.

'I promised that we would have your favourite dish the next time we dined together. Who would have thought it would be under such circumstances?'

'You would. You had this planned all the time.'

'Oh, no. Not until you threw down the gauntlet. I had no choice but to take it up. You insulted me, and you couldn't be allowed to get away with it.'

'Aren't you ashamed of yourself, seeking revenge?' she challenged. 'Only petty men do that.'

He laughed. 'In your country, maybe. But here a man who doesn't take revenge for an insult cannot hold up his head.'

'On a woman?'

He shrugged. 'The insult came from a woman. And, since a thousand women cannot be the equal of one man, a man who lets himself be bested by a woman is truly disgraced.'

She was about to explode when she saw his eyes twinkling at her, as though he knew exactly what she expected, and was playing up to it. And she remembered just what a very clever man Ali was. She was moving through a strange dream, where every reference was moved, the impossible became real and the solid ground dissolved beneath her feet. And he understood it all.

As he had done the first night, he handed her to her seat, and served her himself.

'It's a good thing your servants can't see you doing that,' she observed. 'I'm sure it's beneath your dignity to serve a woman.'

'*Touché*. But, as you are constantly reminding me, you are like no other woman.'

'No, I'm worth a good deal more, aren't I?' she riposted, remembering a grievance. 'I gather thirty thousand is the going rate.'

'Ah, yes, you've met my cousin. He's an engaging rascal, but he has no sense of responsibility. He acts first and thinks afterwards. He'd like me to give him a share in running the country, but he'll have to grow up first. It was improper of him to force himself on you this morning.'

'And see me without my veil; don't forget that.' She added primly, 'I nearly fainted with horror.'

He laughed at her irony. 'Yes, I guessed your delicate sensibilities would be offended.'

'My sensibilities were offended by discovering that you've let everyone think that a hundred thousand was my purchase price, as though I were one of your racehorses.'

'Certainly not!' Ali said, shocked. 'A first-class racehorse costs far more than that.'

Fran threw up her hands in despair. 'There's no talking to you.'

He grinned and filled her wine glass.

For the moment she gave up trying to bring him to a sense of his iniquity. The food was splendid, she knew she looked beautiful, and she was with the most attractive man she had ever met. It was useless to deny that, even if he was her enemy. And it was hard to think of him as an enemy when his eyes danced at her over his glass and told her that she entranced him.

'Come,' he said, when they had finished eating. 'I have something for you to see.'

He took her hand and led her to a chest that stood near the window. He flung it open and she gasped at the treasure that lay within. Rubies, emeralds, diamonds, pearls, gold and silver lay there, jumbled together.

Ali lifted a necklace of emeralds set in gold and held it up before her eyes.

'You have the kind of colouring that can wear all jewels,' he said. 'Diamonds and pearls, as well as rubies and emeralds. Today I think it will be emeralds; tomorrow—'

'Nothing,' Fran said. 'Neither today nor tomorrow. I won't take anything from you, Ali, because I have nothing to give back.'

She looked at him levelly. She wanted no misunderstanding.

He sighed. 'Why do you fight what is between us?'

'Because I'm here by force. As long as I'm a prisoner, there is nothing between us.'

'You're a hard, unforgiving woman—'

'I'm a *free* woman.' She tapped her breast. 'Free in

my heart, where it counts. In here I have something that you'll never conquer by force or trickery.'

Before she could say more the door was flung open and someone strode into the room. Fran started at the sight of Prince Yasir. His face was flushed, and he seemed on the verge of losing control.

Ali's face darkened, and he said something in Arabic that sounded like a command. Yasir replied in the same tongue, obviously furious. He pointed to Fran, and held up two, then three fingers. She stared at him, wondering if she'd understood properly, and which of them she was angrier with if she had.

Ali was clearly giving a refusal, and Yasir's temper increased. Ali made a gesture of finality. Yasir pointed at Fran and held up four fingers.

'You do and you're dead!' she muttered.

'Don't worry,' Ali replied coolly. 'When I sell you, I shall demand much more than four times the original price.'

'How much?' Yasir demanded at once. 'For her I pay whatever you ask.'

He reached for Fran, who drew back a fist in readiness. But Ali was there before her. The next moment Yasir was reeling back against the wall, rubbing his chin.

Ali gave him no chance to recover. Seizing Yasir's collar, he hauled him to the door and threw him out. He turned back into the room before the look in his eyes had changed, and Fran backed away, astounded at what she saw there. Ali was ready to commit murder.

In two steps he was beside her, pulling her into his arms.

'He dared to offer me money for you,' he grated. 'He thinks money can buy anything.'

'Not me,' she said breathlessly. 'Neither his nor yours.'

She wasn't sure that he heard her. His eyes were searching her with the brooding intensity of a man who'd seen a prize almost snatched from him, but had recovered it in time.

'From the moment I first saw you I knew you had to be mine,' he murmured. 'I can wait no longer.'

She stiffened in alarm. She had resolved not to yield, and if she didn't assert herself now it would be too late.

'Ali, let me go,' she breathed.

'Never in life. You're mine, and you'll be mine for ever.'

The prospect was seductively sweet. For a moment her senses swam. To give him all of herself on a tide of passion, if only...

Putting out all her strength, she broke from him and turned away quickly.

'This isn't going to happen,' she gasped.

Ali's eyes kindled as he reached for her, and Fran knew he was at danger point. There was only one thing to do. Throwing caution to the winds, she fended him off and boxed his ears hard enough to make his eyes water.

It was safe to assume that no woman had ever treated his royal person in such a way before. Ali was motionless through sheer astonishment.

'You forced me,' Fran said breathlessly.

'You—'

'Don't look at me like that.' She swiftly put a table

between them. 'It was your own fault for not acting like a gentleman.'

'I don't have to be a gentleman,' he snapped. 'I'm the prince.'

'That's where you're wrong. The prince should always be a gentleman.'

Ali breathed hard. 'You picked a wonderful time to start lecturing me. Your recklessness will lead you into trouble one day.'

'One day? What do you think this is? So now what happens? Do I get thrown into a dungeon for daring to strike the prince?'

'Don't tempt me,' Ali said through gritted teeth. He turned sharply away, less he see the confusion in his eyes as he brought his temper under control. When he felt he could speak calmly he turned back and regarded her with frosty eyes.

'*Now* will you release me?' Fran demanded.

'Release you?' he echoed in amazement. 'After this?' He took a long, hard breath. 'Much as I would like to let you feel the full weight of my displeasure, I have to approach the matter more subtly. Tomorrow you will be taken to a different apartment.'

'Aha!' she said triumphantly. 'The dungeon!'

Ali gritted his teeth. 'Your new apartment will be of the greatest comfort and luxury. You will have eight maidservants with instructions to attend to your every whim. Wherever you go, people will bow. I shall shower you with jewels, which you will wear at all times.'

'What is this?' Fran demanded suspiciously. 'If you're hoping to change my mind, let me tell you—'

'From this moment you are my official favourite,

entitled to the special treatment of one who has exerted herself to please me.'

'But I didn't exert myself to please you. Nor will I, ever!'

'Well, if you think I want the world knowing *that*—!' he said savagely.

Fran stared at him, her jaw dropping as the implications of this washed over her.

'Oh, my goodness!' she breathed. 'You're caught, aren't you? You can't let anyone suspect that Prince Ali Ben Saleem had his face slapped by a woman he'd deigned to honour.' She gave a peal of laughter.

'If you don't stop that,' he grated, 'I really will throw you into a dungeon.'

'No, you won't,' she choked. 'It would give too much away. And after you paid all that money for me you wouldn't want people to know that your judgement was slipping. Oh, heavens! This is wonderful!'

'That's enough!' There was real menace in his eyes this time. 'You're very sure of yourself, but suppose I decided to dispense with your consent? Who do you think would help you?'

She met his eyes, unafraid, defiant. 'You won't do that.'

'Let me remind you who I am, and what my powers are.'

'But that's why you won't,' she said breathlessly. 'It would be an admission of failure, an admission that you can't win me. Nobody else might know, but you and I would, and you couldn't live with that.'

His face was black with anger and she knew she'd touched a nerve.

'And there's another reason,' she added. 'You couldn't do it. You're a tyrant, a scheming manipulator and an arrogant, conceited dictator, but you're fundamentally a decent man, and it isn't in you.'

He regarded her. The fury had died out of his face but his eyes were still unforgiving.

'You have the tongue of a serpent,' he said bitterly. 'Let me warn you that a woman who can discern a man's weaknesses should have the good sense not to taunt him with them.'

'So you admit you have weaknesses? Well, that's a step in the right direction.'

'Does nothing make you afraid?' he snapped.

'Would I tell you?'

'Even you have weaknesses.'

'But perhaps I'm better at keeping them hidden.'

Ali breathed hard. 'To think that I—' He checked himself, on the verge of putting something into words that shocked him.

'That you what?'

'Nothing. But one day I shall have sons. And I shall tell them about women like you, and warn them to avoid such women like scorpions.'

'Pity someone didn't warn you,' Fran said affably. 'I think I'll be going now. Will you summon the bearers?'

'Are you mad?' he demanded. 'You can't leave before morning or the whole palace will know.'

'And your reputation will be shot to pieces,' she teased.

'Do you realise that you've condemned us to a night of making small talk?'

'You could give me that interview.'

'Be very careful!'

'All right, then I'm going to sit down and finish my

supper. And why shouldn't we make small talk? I'll bet you've never done that with a woman before.'

'Nonsense.'

'It isn't nonsense. You only have two attitudes to women—seductive and dismissive. But you can't seduce me and for a few hours you can't dismiss me, so you'll have to talk to me properly, about something that really matters.'

'I've told you I don't do that with women.'

'Exactly my point. So we seem to be faced with a long, boring night, chatting about the weather.'

He merely scowled and seated himself. When Fran poured him some wine he scowled again, but accepted it. She had a sudden conviction that he was longing to rub his cheek, but would die rather than let her see him do it.

Her lips twitched. On the face of it nothing had changed. She was still Ali's prisoner, subject to his power. But she had challenged that power, and discovered its limits, and her confidence was coming back.

CHAPTER SEVEN

'TELL me some more about Yasir,' Fran suggested.

'His father was my father's brother—his elder brother, unfortunately, so Yasir thinks that his father should have taken the throne, instead of mine.'

'Doesn't the eldest son take over automatically?'

'No. This part of the world is dangerous, and a ruler must be strong. My father was the stronger, so he took the throne as was his right. But Yasir feels that he, not I, should rule, and the result is a scene such as you saw tonight, for which I apologise. He had no right to burst in here, and I shall make sure he knows it.'

'I think he already does. Were you wise to strike him?'

'Most unwise. Luckily he's a good-natured fellow, and will forgive me easily.'

Fran decided to say no more. But she had seen a burning resentment in Yasir's expression that told her Ali had misread his cousin. She became thoughtful.

As she watched Ali's scowling countenance an imp of mischief was taking possession of her. It might be reckless and unwise, but that was in her nature. She'd never run from a risk.

'Something amuses you?' Ali growled.

'I was just thinking about the fix you're in.'

'Then I advise you to keep your amusement to yourself.'

'All right, I've got an idea. Let's go back to the

beginning, and talk as we might have done that first night, if I could have told you everything.'

'I thought you told me a good deal,' Ali said. He added with a touch of bitterness, 'But of course it was all invented—all those pretty stories about the Arabian nights were planted, because you thought they would entice me to indiscretions that you could make use of.'

'Oh, no,' she said quickly. 'That was all true. I told you things about myself I've never told anyone else, and I'd hate you to think—that, at least, was real. Please, Your Highness, you must believe me.'

He gave a twisted smile. 'I think we've got a little beyond "Your Highness".' This time he did rub his cheek, and actually managed to return her smile. There was a touch of ruefulness in his eyes that almost made her start to like him again. Almost. She must guard against his charm, she told herself.

'I told you those things because I knew you'd understand. Nobody else ever could. Uncle Dan and Aunt Jean thought only solid things mattered. They didn't have any time for "fancy ideas". At school I took supposedly useful, worthwhile subjects, like mathematics and computing, because they wanted me to. And when I turned out to be good at them I was kind of set on my path for ever. After that nobody ever thought of me as having a fanciful side—until you.

'It was a glorious release, being able to talk about those things after all these years. It was like somebody opened a door.'

'Yes,' Ali said quietly. He wished she wouldn't say these things that reminded him of his own feelings that night. The certainty that he'd found a sympathetic soul, able to understand him without words, had almost overwhelmed him. Suddenly his loneliness—the loneliness of a man who had everything except that which he truly wanted—had seemed to fade.

They had said very little, but that little had opened up long vistas of understanding. Her beauty and sexual charisma had heightened her magic, but been only a small part of it. He had ached to take her into his bed, but also into his heart.

When he'd been called away on business, he had cursed inwardly, and cut the call as short as he dared. But he'd never doubted that this woman whose soul spoke to his own would be waiting, still held in the enchantment that was woven around them both.

When he'd found her gone, it had been as though she'd punched him in the heart. He'd had no experience of rejection, and he'd felt like a young boy, floundering to get his bearings. He'd been compelled to hide his feelings and laugh it off, lest his servants suspect that a woman had mocked the Prince of Kamar. It had been a lesson in reality, and like all the lessons of his life it had taken place in a cruel spotlight.

Later, of course, he'd understood that she had never meant to go through with it. When she'd reappeared as a journalist he'd realised that it was a set-up from start to finish.

And now here she was, ostensibly in his power, yet still teasing and challenging him, still leaving him empty-handed. A man couldn't win with this woman, and that was something he had to alter.

Fran was still talking, apparently oblivious to his mood.

'After that it was just taken for granted that I'd go on taking useful subjects because I was good at them. So I went to college and did economics, which I must admit was fascinating.

'You wouldn't think stocks and shares and financial forecasts could be as thrilling as all that, but they were. And when I discovered that I had a "nose" for the markets that sealed my fate. I've got a friend who never buys new shares without calling to ask what I think.'

'Indeed!' Ali said coldly. 'A little more wine?'

'No, thank you. I want to tell you what they say about your companies on the Stock Exchange.'

'I'm not interested in what a woman has to say about my companies, or the London Stock Exchange.'

'I can tell you what they're saying in Wall Street too,' Fran went on, unperturbed, 'and the Bourse in France.'

'But I have no wish to hear.'

'I'm sure you haven't. But there's not a lot you can do about it, is there?' she asked lightly.

'You are making a big mistake,' he informed her.

Instead of answering in words Fran extended her index finger and beckoned to him. Her smile was enticing and her eyes full of mischief. Ali felt his head swim, and before he knew what he was doing he had leaned towards her. Fran came closer, and when she spoke her warm breath whispered against his face.

'It's very simple, my darling,' she murmured. 'If you don't let me say what I want, *and* pay attention, I shall scream for help at the top of my voice.'

'And do you think anyone will come?'

'Of course not. But they'll hear, and they'll know that you paid a hundred thousand for nothing.'

Ali drew a long breath, a prey to conflicting emotions. The skittering of her breath on his face was sending tremors through him, causing reactions that infuriated him. It was maddening to know that this woman could make him want her to madness as the very moment she was mocking him. She must be resisted and taught a lesson.

But she had called him 'my darling'.

'You,' he said with deliberation, 'are descended from a rattlesnake. Your father was a vulture. A man foolish enough to love you will end up with his heart shrivelled and his bones bleached white in the desert.'

'And you,' she returned, 'are making a big mistake in trusting Lemford Securities. The man who runs it lives on the edge. He's borrowing short and lending long, and I'm sure you know that's a recipe for disaster. Or don't you? Well, let me explain—'

'I can follow that kind of kindergarten economics,' he snapped.

'I'm so glad, because then maybe you can understand the rest.'

'I'm warning you—'

'And I'm warning you that the man in charge of your Wall Street operation isn't what he seems. He's changed his name several times to hide his involvement in some very dubious operation—'

'I have men whose job it is to discover this kind of information—'

'Then fire them, because they're letting you down. Take this.'

She took out the notebook that had been returned to her. Ali regarded her grimly.

'I never travel without it,' she told him, tearing off a sheet on which were written some internet addresses and giving it to him.

'Visit these sites,' she said. 'You'll learn enough about him to alarm you. But *you* do it. Don't delegate to someone else.' She was too absorbed in what she was saying to realise that she'd fallen into her efficient 'business' voice. But Ali realised it, and he bristled.

'Do you have any further orders for me?' he asked frostily.

'Don't you dare come the heavy sheikh with me,' she warned him. 'If you do what I say, I've just saved you a fortune.' She couldn't resist adding, 'Much more than my purchase price.'

'I wish you'd stop talking as though I'd bought you like a commodity.'

'It's the impression you strove to give. I'm merely taking up where you left off.'

Ali took the paper, meaning to toss it contemptuously away. But he didn't, and at heart he knew he wasn't going to.

Fran was too wise to press her point any further, and they finished the meal in light, meaningless conversation.

'It is late and you will be tired,' he observed, leading her into the room where his great bed stood. His eyes met hers. 'Nobody will disturb you.'

She almost had a moment of regret as she saw him walk away into a small side room. The door opened just enough to reveal that this was an office. Then it closed, shutting her out.

The bed was so large and so empty even when she lay down. It was a bed made for passion, where two people could forget the world in each other. And deep inside part of her wanted to do exactly that with this intriguing, fascinating and disturbing man. But it must not be. Not yet. Perhaps not ever.

She lay worrying at this dismaying thought, until she went to sleep.

He woke her as the sun was rising. He looked tired,

like a man who'd spent all night in front of a computer and on the telephone. He didn't volunteer anything, but she thought she detected a new look of respect in his eyes.

'Your bearers will be here in a moment,' he said, 'and they will return you to your quarters for the last time. Later today you will be escorted to your new apartments.'

He took her hand to lead her to the litter.

'Don't think this is the end of the matter,' he said. 'Our battle has moved onto new ground, but it is far from over. You're not as cold as you want me to think. Before I have finished, you will beg for my love.'

'In your dreams,' she said softly, and the bearers arrived before he could reply.

All that day the palace was in a bustle. Everyone knew that the prince had taken his new concubine to his bed, and enjoyed a night of passion with her such as no man had known before. Rumour said that this western woman was possessed of exotic arts that had won his heart and soul, and no reward was too great for her.

Nobody knew her true identity, but that was unimportant, as the prince's favourite had no life beyond his pleasure. He had decreed that henceforth she would be known as the Lady Almas Faiza.

Leena explained to Fran that Almas meant diamond, and Faiza meant victorious. Fran brooded over the intriguing word. Was Ali saying that she had scored a victory over him, or referring to the victory he was determined to have over her? But he had hinted also that they would find victory together, and, try as she might, Fran couldn't escape a thrill of anticipation at the thought of that joint victory.

With awe the servants prepared the lavish apartments that were kept for the favourite. The mosaics
were washed, the floors polished, all the hangings
were replaced, and the air was sweetly scented.

Finally came the ceremony without which her status
would not be official. A litter was brought to her door.
It was unlike the other one, in that it had no curtains
or roof, for in this one she must be seen.

Gorgeously dressed and veiled, she seated herself
and was raised high in the air on the shoulders of her
bearers. Four maids positioned themselves in front and
four behind. Two of them bore large bowls, piled with
jewels. The favourite held out one graceful hand, and
two snow-white doves fluttered out and settled on her
arm. Rasheeda placed herself at the head of the pro-
cession and cried out something in Arabic, which Fran
now knew meant, 'She who has been honoured ap-
proaches.' Then they were moving.

Right through the palace they travelled, through
long corridors, broken by horseshoe arches, decorated
with mosaics, inlaid with gold. Everywhere she looked
there was gold, silver, mother-of-pearl. The ceilings
were high and often lit by windows above, so that the
atmosphere was pleasantly cool and light.

Then it was time to go into the first courtyard,
which, although enclosed, was almost as large as a
garden, filled with flowers and small trees. Here were
the children of the many palace officials, with their
mothers and nurses. They all laughed and greeted her,
and the children tossed sweets which landed on her
satin cushions.

At the far side of the courtyard they re-entered the
palace. Men appeared bearing gifts, which the maids
graciously accepted on her behalf. The gifts were of

the finest and most costly, for everyone wanted to show their respect for Sheikh Ali by honouring his favourite.

Fran's eyes opened wide at the sight of a delicate sherbet set, made of gold and multicoloured glass, set on a gold tray. Behind this came a huge bowl of the finest porcelain, then a perfume bottle encrusted with rubies.

The second courtyard was smaller, dominated by a large fountain in the centre. There was nobody here, but, looking up, Fran saw that all the windows were crowded with spectators.

Then it was back into the palace, where more people came out to stare, and bow low as she passed.

I don't believe this is happening to me, she thought.

At last they reached her own apartments, opposite the prince's. Here Ali himself was waiting, and in the sight of them all he inclined his head to her. For such a woman even the ruler made a gesture of reverence. And only the woman on the litter and the man waiting to receive her knew the true irony of the situation.

He handed her down from the litter, and she lowered her head to him very slightly. Her mind was full of a multitude of images, too many to understand at once, but she saw that she was facing a magnificent trio of floor-length windows, all in the shape of horse-shoe arches.

'Allow me to show you your personal garden,' Ali said, leading her through the centre window.

Outside was truly a place of wonder. Awed by its beauty, she accompanied Ali along the paths between the four fountains, exclaiming over the peacocks and gazelles that wandered freely. Courtiers remained at a respectful distance, speculating on what the prince was saying to his lady, and she to him, and why they both smiled.

They would have been astonished to overhear the conversation.

'You bowed to me,' Ali murmured. 'My round, I think.'

'Nonsense!' she replied. 'You bowed to me first. I was just returning the courtesy.'

'The prince does not bow to a woman.'

'Nevertheless, you did.'

Turning her head, she was just in time to catch him doing the same thing. Unmistakably his lips twitched. The next moment he was staring ahead again, the model of propriety.

Among the spectators there was some interest as to how the lady would react to the prince's gift of welcome. Instead of a rivière of diamonds, or something equally fabulous, he had chosen to give her a carpet. It was a very nice carpet, the best to be had. But it was a strange choice, and they wondered if the favourite would be disappointed.

Instead, they saw her give a trill of laughter, and throw her arms about the prince's neck. His own laughter mingled with hers as he said, 'I wondered if you would understand.' That remark baffled the onlookers.

Sitting alone in her apartments that evening—alone, that was, except for her personal attendants, her hairdresser, her chief confectioner and her private chef—Fran regarded that carpet. It didn't fly, but apart from that it was exactly like the one of her dreams.

Her surroundings vanished and she was back again

in Ali's London house, telling him of her childhood dreams.

'...a flying carpet was going to come through the window and carry me off...'

She would never forget his reply. 'I think that for you the carpet will come.'

Neither of them could have foreseen this day, yet when the moment had come he'd known exactly what to give her. It strengthened her suspicion that Ali had secretly lured her here to fulfil her Arabian nights fantasy.

She smiled at the thought, but then the smile faded. Her attraction to him was powerful, real, and no part of a fantasy. It was like a holiday, except that Ali had compelled her to take it, because that was how he did things. But afterwards?

She wasn't the kind of woman who could be sent on her way with a few glamorous memories and gifts. If she loved, it would be for real, and not as part of a holiday fantasy.

Whatever she felt about Ali, and he felt about her, they wouldn't discover it in this place.

There was a small flutter near the door, and she turned to find Leena standing there. 'Prince Yasir begs your permission to approach.'

He was as meek as a schoolboy, but his eyes danced.

'I come to offer you my tribute,' he said. 'If, in your justified anger, you reject it, I shall be so ashamed that I shall ride into the desert and never be seen again.'

'Don't talk foolishness,' she laughed.

'Say that you forgive me for my unforgivable behaviour yesterday,' he begged outrageously.

'I shouldn't.'

'I know. But do it anyway. See what I have brought you.'

His gift was a lavishly jewelled sash, which oddly jarred her. It was too much. But this was a country of too much, she reflected, and perhaps this was his way of atoning. She smiled and praised the sash, and when he displayed considerable relief she felt that she had been right.

He accepted her invitation to tea and they were soon chatting like old friends.

'I expect Ali told you our family history,' Yasir said ruefully. 'Of course I have the greatest respect for him as our country's ruler, but I can't resist the temptation to tweak his nose now and then. He knows it doesn't mean anything, and I hope that you do too.'

'I'd like to believe it meant nothing,' she said, 'but when I saw you fighting, and your look when he struck you—'

He laughed merrily. 'We've been scrapping since we were boys. Sometimes we fight, sometimes we race. Ali has some wonderful horses, but mine are better.'

'Arab steeds!' she exclaimed. 'I've heard of them. They're said to be the finest horses in the world.'

'You should get Ali to show you his beauties. Can you ride?'

'Sort of. I learned on a farm when I was a child. But the pony was a bit slow.'

'Tell Ali you want to ride his best mares. If he's too mean to agree I'll let you ride one of mine.'

He gave her a cheery wave and departed, leaving her thoughtful. Leena reminded her that she hadn't finished ordering the evening meal, and it was important to serve what pleased His Highness. Luckily the chef knew what would please His Highness far better than Fran did, and she was able to leave the matter to him.

Ali arrived in thoughtful mood that evening. He enjoyed the meal, and thanked her courteously for paying so much attention to his requirements, but she could tell that there was something on his mind, and she thought she knew what it was.

'Yasir came to see me today,' she said. 'He wanted to apologise and bring me a gift—that jewelled sash over there.'

Ali examined it and grunted. 'Do you like this?'

'Not really. I think it's overdone, but I didn't like to hurt his feelings by saying so.'

'It's like Yasir to go a little further than he needs, but I'm glad he is showing you the proper respect at last.'

'Have you made your peace with him?'

'You mean has he made his peace with me?'

'Yes, of course.'

'He's apologised, and I've told him to behave himself in future. He asked my permission to visit you and I gave it, feeling certain you were now safe from his advances.'

'He didn't come within three feet of me,' she assured him.

'It would have surprised me if he had. He's fond of harking back to the past, reminding me that his father was the elder brother. I reminded him that in those days he could have been beheaded for what he did. In view of his contrition, you have my permission to receive him.'

'Thank you,' she said ironically. 'You're very poor company tonight. Yasir was far more entertaining.'

'May I ask why?' Ali enquired coolly.

'He told me of his horses. He said I should ask you to let me ride one of your best mares, and if you're too mean I can ride his.'

'There will be no need for that. My animals are at your disposal. We can travel to Wadi Sita whenever you wish.'

'Wadi Sita?' she echoed, trying to sound indifferent.

She knew the name well. Wadi Sita was the legendary oasis that no journalist had ever penetrated. Here Ali indulged himself in exotic orgies of pleasure, safely hidden from the world's prying eyes. And now he had invited her there. But he would withdraw the invitation if he knew her eagerness, so she kept all trace of it out of her voice.

'Sita is the Arabic word for six,' he explained. 'Wadi means a valley, usually a pleasant valley with trees and water. We have six such places in the Kamar desert, but Wadi Sita is my favourite. I shall mount you on Safiya. She is my best mare, white as milk, light and strong, but gentle.'

'It sounds wonderful. When can we leave?'

'Tomorrow.' He rose. 'I'll give orders immediately. In fact, I won't be back tonight at all. I have urgent matters to attend to.'

His eyes met hers, and he nodded slightly.

'I heeded your warning. I checked, as you said.'

'And you discovered that your men were letting you down.'

Ali's lips twisted in bitterness. 'Worse. They were engaged in an active conspiracy to steal from me. They are being brought here now to be questioned about the money they've taken—how much, and where it's hidden. That will occupy me for the next few hours.'

'Suppose they won't talk?'

His eyes were as bleak as a steel wall. 'They will,' he said simply, and Fran knew a fleeting moment of pity for those who had dared to cross Ali Ben Saleem.

He paused, and she could tell that the next words cost him an effort. 'I am in your debt for revealing their dishonesty.'

Fran smiled, but was too tactful to say anything.

'Thank you,' Ali said jerkily, and went away.

CHAPTER EIGHT

THEY left for Wadi Sita late the following afternoon, when the sun was already sinking. A helicopter took them direct from the roof of the palace to a landing pad in the oasis itself.

Fran spent the journey glued to the window, watching for her first glimpse of the famous oasis. At last Wadi Sita came in sight. Far below she could make out the glitter of water, palm trees and beautiful gardens. Surrounding this was what seemed to be a small town, with a few buildings and many tents.

'When in the desert I like to live simply,' Ali explained. 'So we live in tents.'

Because the oasis was so small they were met not by a car, but by Ali's favourite stallion, and also a dainty white mare for Fran, so beautiful that she cried out with delight.

'She is called Safiya, which means patient,' Ali told her.

Safiya lived up to her name. She had large, beautiful eyes, was silken-mouthed and moved with a soft, gliding step. Fran immediately felt safe on her back.

It was still very warm, but the sun was no longer at furnace heat, and a pleasant breeze sprang up. Fran glanced at Ali, enjoying the sight of him on his black horse. He rode proudly, with his head up, his white burnouse fluttering in the breeze, and the sunset gleaming off the gold cords that held it in place.

He glanced in her direction, and she quickly looked

away, dismayed to have been caught looking at him. She had an uneasy notion that she'd been smiling at the magnificent picture he presented, which might mislead him into thinking that she was weakening.

Looking around, she noticed a high building, larger than the others, where every window was covered with bars. They were elegant and ornate, and the last of the sun turned the brass to gold, making them beautiful. But still, this was obviously some kind of prison.

'You've noticed my harem,' Ali said casually. 'I keep a special one out here for the sake of convenience. My raiders travel far and wide kidnapping women who are kept locked up there, awaiting my pleasure.'

'What?' Then Fran noticed that he was grinning. 'You—!'

'I couldn't resist it. You're so ready to believe every tall tale about me.'

'There wouldn't be any tall tales if you came clean.'

'Why should I? I'm not accountable to the world for what I do in my own country.'

'Of all the arrogant—!'

He laughed aloud. 'You goose, that's the Water Extraction Company. The water here is rich in minerals and sulphur, and has unique properties for curing many ailments.

'The company works on finding new cures. But we have to look out for industrial spies. Several major drug companies have tried to steal our discoveries, so that they can patent them before we can do so ourselves. Then they could charge extortionate prices, whereas I only want a reasonable profit for my country. So the bars are part of the security arrangements.'

He glanced at her, his lips twitching. 'You're not

taking notes,' he complained. 'Of course, this isn't as interesting as the tales of the wicked sheikh who makes love to fifty women a night.'

'Only fifty? I'd heard a hundred.'

'No, no, I'm only human.'

She burst out laughing and he joined her.

At last they reached the edge of the oasis, where there was a village of tents, bounded by palm trees, and, beyond them, the desert. Darkness had fallen, but the village was lit by flaming torches held high by a hundred arms, illuminating a path as the Sheikh and his favourite rode side by side in majesty.

When they reached her tent he lifted her down himself, holding her high for a moment before lowering her slowly against his chest. Then he kissed her before all the world, and all the world cheered.

Her tent was a mini palace, thickly carpeted, hung with silken drapes and lavishly provided with huge cushions. Partitions divided it into rooms, one for eating, one for sleeping, one for washing away the hot dust. Her maids were already there, having been sent on ahead to prepare.

When she had bathed and Leena had anointed her with sweet-smelling oils, there was the serious process of deciding what to wear for the evening. Leena displayed several garments, but gently nudged her towards one of white and saffron, against which her skin glowed warmly.

Ali's eyes, too, glowed, when he saw her. He had come to fetch her for the feast that was to be given in her honour.

'Tonight we eat under the stars,' he said. 'And because this is an informal place there is no need for your veil. Many tribesmen are here. They are my friends, and they have come for miles across the desert for a glimpse of you.'

'But we only planned this trip last night. How did they know to make the journey?'

'For a woman who prides herself on being modern, you ask some remarkably silly questions. Even tribesmen have mobile phones these days.'

He took her hand and led her out of the tent. Fran's first thought was that the place had caught fire. Men stood as far as the eye could see, each carrying a torch. She put her head up and smiled.

Ali led her to two huge cushions, and they sat together, cross-legged, and presided over the feast. All the finest foods were spread before them, in such profusion that Fran felt giddy.

This was followed by the entertainment. A large space was cleared and suddenly the air was filled with whoops and yells. A troop of horsemen burst onto the scene, galloping around and around in a circle, performing amazing acrobatics. Ali explained that they were tribesmen who still lived in the desert and treasured the skills handed down from their ancestors.

There had never been such riders, doing handstands on the backs of fast galloping horses, leaping from horse to horse, landing perfectly every time. With each landing there were yells and yodels of triumph, until the air was filled with their cries.

Finally there came one horseman on his own. He was better dressed than the others and his face was covered, except for his eyes. He was the least skilled, but the crowd roared and cheered as if he was a star, and Fran understood why when he landed at her feet and revealed himself to be Yasir.

'What are you doing here, playing the fool?' Ali demanded cheerfully.

'I came to pay my respects,' Yasir said, sweeping an extravagant bow to Fran. She smiled and applauded, and he vanished into the crowd.

A young man appeared with a lyre, and began to sing. Fran didn't understand the words, but the music, with its poignant sound of happiness that was half sadness, seemed to take possession of her. Ali leaned close and whispered, 'It is an Arabic poem, hundreds of years old. It means, "My heart rides with the wild wind, my steed is fast, my love rides by my side..."'

'That's beautiful,' Fran said.

'"The wind is eternal,"' Ali continued. '"The sand is eternal. Our love is eternal."'

The singer's voice grew melancholy.

'"She is gone from me. But, in my heart, we shall ride in the moonlight, for ever,"' Ali translated. 'Come, my love, let us walk together.'

He took her hand, and the crowds melted away. He led her to the gardens where they could walk under the palm trees, watched through the leaves by parrots, and listen to the soft plashing of the fountains.

'This is such a perfect place,' she murmured.

'I hoped you would think so. I believe the Enchanted Gardens must be like this.'

'The Enchanted Gardens?' she echoed. 'Where are they?'

'Anywhere you like. They are where lovers meet when the storms and stress of life are over. Or they exist in your heart. My father built this garden as a gift for my mother. We all have our own Enchanted Gardens. Mine are with you.'

He kissed her tenderly, and led her away down

winding paths to where the desert began, and the brilliant moon threw black shadows among the dunes.

'Here it is,' he said, 'the desert you dreamed of. And tomorrow I shall show it to you. We shall leave very early in the morning, while it is cool and pleasant, and return when the sun climbs. At midday you will sleep, and in the evening we shall venture out again. Perhaps we shall ride on for ever, and never be seen again by human eyes. And the desert, which is so full of mysterious legends, will have another one.'

'When you talk such beautiful nonsense I could almost wish it to happen,' she whispered.

'It's a crime to accuse the prince of talking nonsense,' he told her with a smile.

'Beautiful nonsense,' she reminded him.

'Then I forgive you. There is much beauty for me to show you, but the greatest beauty of all is in you.'

She had never known him speak so simply and gently before, and her heart responded with joy. He drew her close and she went gladly into his arms. His kiss was like his speech, loving, almost reverent, not demanding but coaxing, and it was irresistible.

'Ali,' she whispered, melting against him.

'Say my name again,' he begged. 'I love to hear it on your lips.'

She said it again, and then again. It had a wonderful sound, until he silenced it by covering her mouth with his own. His lips were warm, firm yet tender. They spoke to her not only of passion, but of love, and something inside her flowered. If only he could always be like this.

She felt him lift her high in his arms and begin to walk back the way they had come. She clung to him, her eyes closed, for she wanted no images to intrude on the fever of longing that possessed her.

He laid her down. They were in darkness except for one small lamp. Fran reached up for him, caressing his face, eager for his love. If he wanted her now, she knew she had no will to refuse him.

But this was a clever man, as subtle as the serpent in the Garden of Eden. Instead of lying down beside her, he kissed her gently and rose again, leaving her longing.

'I shall be here for you before dawn,' he said. 'Be ready for me, for I shall bring a flying carpet to transport you to a magic land.'

Then he was gone, and she was alone, wondering what kind of man this was who always surprised her.

He was as good as his word, arriving in the cool early light, dressed for riding. She too was in riding breeches, which Leena had brought with her.

They mounted the waiting horses and headed out in the cool morning air to a world that belonged to them alone. The desert lay almost in darkness, but there was just enough light to see by, and soon the oasis was far behind them.

The sun climbed fast and the light grew every moment, flooding the land with colour. Ali spurred his horse and it streaked away over the sand. A light touch, and Safiya did the same, carrying her along like the wind until she almost caught up with him. But he went faster and faster, always keeping her at a little distance, until at last he pulled rein and wheeled to face her.

'Do you know where we are?' he asked, smiling.

She looked around and saw that in every direction the sand stretched as far as her eyes could see.

'We're lost,' she cried, bewildered.

'Of course we're not. We rode away from the sun, and we can return by riding towards it. But just for a little while we are alone in the world. And it can be ours, with only the two of us, and nobody else to tell us yea or nay. If we were on the moon together, I think it would be like this.'

'Oh, yes,' she said, looking about her in wonder.

Beneath their feet the sand rippled away in dunes of varying shades of yellow. Above them the blue, cloudless sky plunged down to meet it. She felt drunk with the vivid intensity of the colours.

He slipped an arm about her shoulders, drawing her sideways on Safiya's back so that she leaned against him, and looked searchingly into her face.

'Let us go on for ever,' he said, 'and seek our Enchanted Garden, where there will be no problems or fighting, and we can love each other as fate meant us to.'

'You make it sound so tempting,' she sighed. 'But we can't run away from the world.'

'Lady Almas Faiza, why must you be so serious?'

'Because things can never be as easy for me as for you.'

'Easy? Do you think it's easy for me to be with you day after day, and feel the distance you put between us?'

She shook her head. 'Not I. The distance is there. I only wish—' She checked herself.

'What do you wish?' he asked eagerly.

She touched his face with tender fingers, but shook her head.

He kissed her once more. 'The sun is high, and we must return. Tonight we will make this journey again as the moon rises. I want you to see my desert in all its moods, for you will understand them better than any other.'

She had thought nothing could be more beautiful than the desert at sunrise, but that night she discovered that she was wrong.

As they strolled to where the horses were waiting, Ali said, 'I used to come here as a child, with my parents. I was too young to understand about love, but I knew even then that the bond between them was very rare.

'I remember one night seeing them ride out to-gether, to be alone, leaving me behind. I was jealous because they shared something that excluded me. And I promised myself that one day I too would ride out with my lady under the moon.'

She looked at him quickly, but he laid gentle fingers over her mouth, as if words would spoil this moment.

The full moon was shining brilliant and silver, draining the world of colour, and making the dunes mysterious and unearthly. They rode for a while and when they stopped Fran looked around, listening, wondering if there had ever been a silence like this one.

'Was it like this in your dreams?' Ali asked.

'Yes. The wizard always conjured his spells under the moon, and the desert was always blue-black. But I never dreamed the reality could be so wonderful.'

He said nothing and she turned her head. In the unearthly light she couldn't see his face, only feel his presence, and his hand holding hers. She was conscious of a wonderful contentment. Whatever else happened to her in the future, she would always have this glorious moment with Ali, when he had brought her only beauty and peace.

'Thank you,' she said at last.

He understood her. He turned without a word, and they retraced their steps to the oasis.

Leena was waiting for her with a cool bath. Afterwards Fran walked dreamily towards the bed, lost in some inner dream.

'Tonight I have new oils to make you beautiful for my lord,' Leena said.

She lay down and let the maid draw the soft towel away from her, revealing her nakedness. A delicious aroma began to pervade the air, like nothing she had ever known before. It was full of secrets and spells and it whispered to her of love and desire, of the most delicate eroticism, and unfulfilled yearning.

She thought of Ali, and how she ached for him. It had always been hard to refuse what she wanted as much as he, and now, after their magic moment of communion in the desert, she felt close to him as never before. She lay on her front, her chin on her arms, longing for him.

She felt hands on her shoulders, rubbing the oil softly into her skin with smooth, practised movements. Gradually Fran relaxed and gave herself up to the enjoyment, refusing to spoil it by looking too far ahead. She gave a long, contented sigh.

'I'm glad to know that I'm pleasing you,' said a soft voice.

'Ali!' She half rose and tried to turn, but his hands on her shoulders pressed her gently down again. 'How did you come to be here?'

'I slipped in a moment ago and sent your maid away.'

He was naked to the waist, wearing only riding breeches. But she herself was completely naked, she realised. This was another of his tricks to take shameless advantage of her, and she knew she should be indignant. But it was hard to summon up the proper emotions when his skilled hands were driving away every feeling but pleasure.

'You had no right to do that,' she murmured.

'I know. I'm a terrible fellow. Can you forgive me?'

'Only if you go away at once,' she said, smiling to herself.

'If that is your wish.'

'You mean—you will?' she asked, unable to keep a hint of dismay out of her voice.

'Of course. Just as soon as I have finished. Now lie still while I finish my work.'

She had no inclination to argue further. It was bliss to lie there while his fingers kneaded the back of her neck, her shoulder blades, then her spine. She drew a long, shuddering breath as he softly traced a line down the length of her back and over the curve of her behind.

'You are beautiful, Diamond,' he murmured into her ear. 'As beautiful as I dreamed of you, with a skin of satin, and a shape that is perfection.'

'You shouldn't be looking at my shape,' she chided him half-heartedly.

'How can I not look, when you display it as shamelessly as a nymph?'

He brushed aside her hair and kissed the back of her neck. She hadn't known she was so sensitive in that one particular spot, but her sudden gasp told him everything. He began to trail kisses down the length of her spine to the small of her back, then up again. The pleasure was light and delicate, and she felt herself melting into it, ready for anything that might happen next, but also ready to wait, as long as this delightful feeling continued.

His hands were gentle, turning her onto her back so that he could continue his work. There was witchcraft in his lips and tongue as they trailed lazily across her breasts, with a flickering movement now and then, heightening the sensation just enough to tantalise her.

'I've longed to see you naked,' he whispered against her fevered skin. 'I've dreamed that you would throw away your weapons, wanting me as I want you.'

She didn't dare to tell him just how much she wanted him. Whatever he thought, the battle wasn't over, and soon she must take up her weapons again. But tonight she would yield to her desire. She could fight him, but not her own mounting passion.

She might regret it tomorrow, but at this moment tomorrow was a day that would never come. The gambler, the risk-taker, rose in her, and said that if she never made love with him she would regret it a thousand times more.

He threw off the last of his clothes, and she saw the magnificence of his body, bronze in the lamplight. He was broad of shoulder and long of back, with a straight spine, lean hips and a firm, muscular behind. There was power in his loins. She could sense it in his strong, graceful movements, and it heightened the desire growing in her.

Then his nakedness was pressed against hers. She revelled in his magnificence, the muscular breadth of his shoulders, the long, straight spine, lean, hard hips and powerful thighs.

She could see now how much he wanted her, but he reached for her gently, loving her to desire by slow degrees until he was certain that her passion matched his.

For this he had many skills at his command. He was a subtle lover who knew how the lightest touch could cause a volcano of sensation, and the softest breath send excitement scurrying across her sensitised skin. He knew how to kiss her slowly, lingeringly, giving her time. There was genius in the kisses he bestowed all over her body, so that she was soon in a fever of sensation.

This was love carried to a point of high art. She felt invaded and possessed by him, although he had not yet claimed her, and was still revelling in the enjoyment of her beauty, as though everything he discovered enchanted him.

She could hold off no longer. 'Tell me that you want me,' she implored.

He told her with lips that brushed against her skin. And then he told her with actions that almost made her heart stop with joy. He told her with his hands, caressing her soft, rounded breasts. He told her with his arms which enfolded her against his chest. Finally he told her with his loins, and then she knew it was true.

Like him she'd dreamed of this, but no dream could be as beautiful as the reality. As soon as their bodies were united she knew that it was right. She clasped him in her arms and held him close, sharing his rhythm as the pleasure mounted.

His face was close to hers, smiling, holding her eyes

with his. She could hear him murmuring soft words. They were in Arabic, but she didn't have to understand them to know their meaning. They were the words of a man absorbed in a woman, for whom nothing existed but her. They held passion, adoration, perhaps even true and lasting love.

She tried to answer, but no words would come, only a sigh. Why had she waited so long to be in his arms, when it was where she belonged? She felt her defences falling away. She didn't want to fight him any more, only to be one with him.

Now it was happening, and her brain was telling her to beware the beauty of that oneness, while her heart was telling her that it was what she had been born for.

When she parted from him she wanted to weep, but the moment passed in the gentle pleasure of sleeping in his arms.

In the cool dawn Fran awoke to an unearthly silence. Ali lay naked beside her, on his front, one arm resting lightly across her, his face buried against her shoulder. He was breathing gently in a peaceful, contented sleep, like a man for whom everything in the world was good.

Fran lay staring into the distance, happy, but troubled. At last she knew the truth about herself that she had suspected, and feared. Cool, efficient Frances Callam, who'd always prided herself on her good sense, her rational approach to every situation, was actually a woman who became a slave to her sensations in her lover's arms. His touch, his kiss, could make the real world vanish. In his embrace she had no will but to stay there for ever. And that scared her.

Now she was herself again, passionately loving the

man who lay beside her, but still herself, separate from him, and knowing that this was right. For if she were not separate, what did she have to give him?

He stirred and woke, gazing directly at her, and at something she saw in his eyes she felt her resolve weaken. What did anything matter but being with him?

He touched her cheek. 'Is all well with you, my Lady Almas Faiza?'

'Almost too well,' she whispered.

'How can that be?'

'Because it's dangerous to be so happy.'

'Words. Happiness is every lover's right. You give me such joy. In return, everything I have is yours.'

Now she should demand her freedom, but she put it off. She couldn't bear to spoil this moment.

'I've wondered why you called me Faiza?' she said. 'Whose victory were you celebrating?'

He looked at her with lazy, contented eyes. 'And now you know the answer. Come here, lady, and conquer me again.'

Unable to resist, she did so, and in the sweetness of that loving all fears were forgotten. Their second loving was like their first in ardour, but with a new sense of discovery. They knew each other's bodies and explored them eagerly and with tenderness. Afterwards they fell asleep again. But when Fran awoke the problems were greater than ever, and she knew that they had to be faced.

'What shall we do today?' he murmured. 'The desert again?'

'No, not the desert.'

'What, then, my life?'

She took a deep breath and crossed her fingers.

'Ali, let me go home.'

He stared. 'Let you go? Now? When we have just truly found each other?'

'But what have we found? I can't love you as your prisoner.'

'As long as you love me, does it matter how?'

'It does to me.'

He yawned and stretched. 'I think I will keep you with me for ever. Never speak of leaving me.'

'But—'

'Silence, woman,' he said, drawing her into his arms and covering her mouth.

It was sweet to be there, sweeter still to kiss him and feel his desire. But there was a core of independence in her that wouldn't let her yield. Summoning all her strength, she freed herself from him.

'Come back to me,' he said, laughing and trying to take hold of her again.

'No! Ali, I'm serious. This is beautiful, but it's unreal.'

'Then enjoy it as unreality. But if you must be so serious I will do something to please you. You may visit the Water Company and ask them any questions you like. They will have my orders to tell you everything.'

'Oh, you're so clever,' she breathed. 'Buying me off with titbits.'

'It's what you wanted, isn't it?'

'Yes, but you think you can talk me round so easily.'

He tightened his arms, pulling her hard against his chest.

'What I think is that, while I'm stronger than you, I don't need to talk you round,' he growled.

He spoke humorously, but beneath the teasing it
was still an assertion of power, one step short of out-
right tyranny.

And again he'd managed to confuse her. As a journalist she would give her eye-teeth to get into the
Water Company, and he knew that. It also implied that
he would soon release her to return home and write
her story. So she had nothing to worry about. And
yet...

She knew the next words were unwise, but nothing
could stop her saying them.

'Aren't you afraid that while I'm in there I'll find a
way of escape?'

He released her abruptly and sat up. When he
turned, the change in his face shocked her. It was as
though winter had come.

'If you ever tried to leave me,' he said in a hard
voice, 'I would never forgive you.'

Rising, he pulled on his clothes, and left without
looking at her.

CHAPTER NINE

AT ANY other time the visit to the Water Company would have thrilled Fran. As Ali had promised, everyone had orders to help her, and what she learned about the work was fascinating. Many women worked there, one of whom was deputed to accompany her, and who seemed extremely knowledgeable. Wryly, Fran thought she could hear Ali laughing at her.

But while she listened and smiled, and asked intelligent questions, she couldn't banish the picture of his face as she had seen it that morning, threatening never to forgive her.

She left in the early afternoon and settled in the gardens, writing up her notes. When she'd finished she put her notebook away and wandered about the gardens, watching the play of the fountains, wondering what would happen next. She and Ali should have talked about the problem this morning, but instead, after the most wonderful night of her life, he'd simply silenced discussion like a dictator, and walked out. A shiver went through her at the memory.

She sat on the edge of the largest fountain and leaned over to gaze down into the water. Suddenly another reflection joined hers, and she looked up, smiling, to find Yasir beside her.

'I believe in England you say "a penny for them",' he said merrily.

'That's right.'

'What strange thoughts you must be having to bring

such a melancholy smile to your face. Are you happy or sad?'

'Both,' she said with a sigh.

'I'm a very good listener.'

He led her away from the fountain and they began to stroll down winding paths.

'Isn't Ali treating you right?' Yasir asked sympathetically. 'I'd heard that you please him so well that he piles every luxury onto you.'

'But the thing I want most isn't a luxury,' she protested. 'It's a right. I want my freedom.'

'You seem free enough to me,' he said, looking around. 'I see no guards.'

'Who needs guards in the middle of the desert? Where could I run to?'

'True. But do you really want to run from Ali?'

'Not really,' she admitted. 'If I had my freedom, I'd probably use it to come back to him.'

'But that would be your own choice, so it would be different.'

'Yes, that's it!' she cried. 'You understand. Why can't he?'

'My cousin Ali is a splendid fellow, but when he's got what he wants he thinks that's the end of the matter.'

'I know,' Fran said with feeling. 'And it's never going to be right with us unless I can come to him freely.'

Yasir nodded. 'You two are perfect together. I hate to think of him spoiling it through pigheadedness. I have a little house near here. You can use my telephone to call the British ambassador.'

'Yasir, really? As simple as that?'

'As simple as that. We could go now.'

He took her hand and drew her away down a narrow path. She hurried with him, anxious not to lose this unexpected chance.

Yasir's 'little house' turned out to be a modest palace, overly ornate and generally too much like the rest of him. Fran hurried in after him and looked around for a telephone.

'Up there,' he said, grasping her hand and mounting the stairs.

She could hardly believe that she was going to find a way out at last. She had a brief moment of hesitation. It was tempting to stay here, living a dream of love with Ali, but she knew it was a temptation she must refuse.

'In here,' Yasir said, throwing open a door and drawing her through.

She found herself in an ornate bedroom, heavily hung in crimson brocade. One wall was bare of drapes, covered with knives of all kinds. Swords, daggers, scimitars, curved knives, long narrow knives, short thick knives. The air was heavy with some exotic perfume that Fran found vaguely displeasing, especially when joined to the disagreeable impression made by the weapons. But she had no time to worry about it.

There was a telephone by the bed and she snatched up the receiver.

'How do I call the ambassador?' she asked urgently.

She thought perhaps Yasir hadn't heard her, for he only smiled. Fran put the receiver to her ear, but heard nothing. The phone was dead.

Then she noticed that Yasir was holding the wire in his hand. He had pulled it out of the wall. As she watched, he turned the key in the door.

And now she realised that there was something horrible about his smile.

'I want to call the ambassador,' she said, more firmly than she felt.

'I'm afraid that wouldn't suit me. I prefer that you stay here—with me. Ali can have you back when I've finished. If he still wants you by then. Which is doubtful.'

Why had she ever thought this was a charming young man? Behind the handsome face his eyes were cold and dead.

'You're mad,' she breathed, backing away from him. 'What do you think Ali will do to you?'

'Oh, he'll be very angry at first, but I'll just make myself scarce for a while and he'll forget. Women matter very little in this country, and the idea of two men carrying on a feud because of one is ridiculous.'

'But it's not about that, is it?' she said to keep him talking. 'Not on your side.'

'How clever of you. No, you're just the instrument. Ali will get over this in time, but he'll suffer, and that's what matters. All my life he's taken everything from me, including the throne that ought to be mine. Now I've taken something from him. And I'm going to enjoy it.'

He made a determined move towards her. She backed off. Alarm was rising as she saw the dimensions of the trap she'd walked into. Yasir's apparent good nature was a mask that deceived even Ali. Beneath it was cold hatred, and it was all turned on her.

Yasir was smiling again, a cruel smile, as though he was relishing the fight to come. Fran forced herself to stay calm and stop backing away. Yasir looked at her breast rising and falling, clearly enjoying himself. He didn't see that she had changed the shape of her hand, so that it was balled into a fist except for two fingers. He came close, reached out to grab her.

The next moment he let out a yell of agony as Fran rammed her extended fingers into his solar plexus, with all her force. He doubled up, clutching his middle, his face contorted with pain and outrage.

But he was between her and the door. She was still trapped with a vicious man who no longer cared what he did, as long as he could show his hate.

'You are going to be very sorry for that,' he grated.

'Not as sorry as you'll be when Ali hears,' she said breathlessly.

'He won't care about you once he knows you came with me. You'll be so much waste to be disposed of.'

'You're lying to convince yourself. Ali loves me.'

He was still gasping, but he bared his teeth in a travesty of a grin. 'You westerners with your foolish notions about men and women. Women are playthings, and he knows that as well as any man, whatever he may have told you. He'll tell you himself, always assuming that he bothers to see you again. Now come here.'

Behind her was the wall with the knives. Unable to see what she was doing, she scrabbled and felt a hilt against her fingers. She wrenched, and to her relief it came off easily. Holding Yasir's eyes with her own, she brought it around to the front. It had a long, wicked-looking blade.

'I will use this if I have to,' she said deliberately.

'Don't be a fool,' he sneered. 'I'm a prince and Ali's cousin. Shed my blood and see what your lover does with you. It won't be pleasant.'

She had a terrible fear that he might be right, but she kept her face impassive while she raised the knife to the level of his eyes and thrust it towards him in a series of little jabbing movements. As she'd hoped, he jerked his head back. She kept coming forward, trying to get between him and the door, but she couldn't manage it. It was stalemate. She could keep him off, but not defeat him.

And then she heard a commotion below, the sound of footsteps running upstairs, a man's voice that sounded like Ali's— *Oh, please God!*

Yasir heard it too. His eyes glittered with spite. Moving too fast for her to follow, he grabbed the knife by the thin blade and pulled his hand down it. The next moment there was blood everywhere as the razor edge sliced his arm. He fell back to the floor at the exact moment that the door crashed in, and Ali stood there with a face as black as thunder. Behind him stood two huge men in the uniform of his personal guard.

'Arrest her!' Yasir shrieked. 'She tried to kill me. I'm bleeding to death.'

The guards made as if to move but Ali raised a hand and they fell back. He stood in silence, looking from Fran, stood holding the blood-stained knife, to his cousin.

'Give that to me,' he said to her.

'Ali—listen to me—'

'Give it to me,' he repeated in a voice of deadly quiet.

In despair she handed him the knife. He turned away from her, dropped to his knees beside Yasir, and examined his wound. At last he rose.

'Guards,' he said in a voice that was cold and bleak, 'arrest this man.'

'She's a murderess!' Yasir cried.

'If she had killed you, it would have been no more than you deserve,' Ali said. 'Think yourself lucky that I don't kill you myself. Take him away. Have his wound tended and see that he is watched at all times.'

Yasir set up a howl of rage, but the guards ignored it, raising him and hauling him off.

Fran leaned back against the wall, faint with relief.

'I thought you were going to—'

'You should have known me better,' Ali said. 'But we can talk later. Come.'

He was wearing long, flowing robes. He put an arm about her shoulders, enfolding her in a gesture of protection, and led her out of the house. He held her like that until they reached her tent.

'He only wanted to get me away from you to make you suffer,' she gasped, weeping. 'I took the knife from his wall to fend him off, but I never used it. He cut himself deliberately when he heard your voice. Ali, you must believe me—'

'Hush, I do believe you. He will be punished, never fear.'

'How did you know where I was?'

'Leena saw you speaking to him in the garden. She understood the danger better than you, and fetched me. You are shaking.'

She was trembling violently, from her own actions as much as Yasir's. Ali took her face between his hands.

'You were very foolish to go with him, but you were also wonderful. I am proud of you. My lady is a tigress.'

'I thought you were going to arrest me—'

'Then you did me an injustice. As though I could ever doubt you.'

His trust in her was unbearable. Fran forced herself to say, 'Ali, I have to be honest with you. I went to Yasir's house because I was trying to escape you.'

He stared at her blankly. 'You went from me to him?'

'No, of course not. I went because he told me I could telephone the British ambassador. *Don't look at me like that!* You knew I wanted to get away.'

'You—meant to leave me? Using the help of that creature?'

'I didn't know what he was like or I wouldn't have gone with him,' she cried. 'What was I to do? Ali, this has to end; I must leave here.'

'After last night—the closeness we discovered?'

'It's because of last night.'

'Are you saying I was wrong?' he asked in disbelief. 'That I only imagined what happened to us in each other's arms?'

'No, you didn't imagine it, but—this place is unreal. I'm not myself here, but somebody else that I don't know. And if I don't know who I am, how do I know what I have to give you?'

Looking into his face, she saw that he didn't understand a word. For all his western ways, Ali was still part of a culture where it didn't matter who—or what—the woman was, as long as she pleased the man. Fran's ideas about giving herself in freedom had no meaning for him.

'Ali, please try to understand,' she begged. 'This has to stop. It's been wonderful but—it's time for me to leave.'

To her dismay, his face hardened. 'That is for me to say.'

'But it's madness to think we can go on like this. Can't you see that—?'

'I see only that it's for me to make the decisions. I will not be dictated to by you or any other woman.'

'You said if I tried to leave you you'd never forgive me,' Fran cried in desperation. 'Well, I tried. So where does that leave us?'

'It leaves you exactly where you were before,' he said in an iron voice. 'Subject to my wishes. Did you imagine my anger would make me send you away? Don't think it for a moment. If we're enemies, that would make another reason for keeping you here. Do you understand me?'

The cold implacability in his face made his meaning all too clear. Fran shivered.

'I offered you a life as my favourite, honoured by everyone, including myself. And you threw it back in my face,' he said coldly. 'Beware lest you find that the life of a discarded favourite is even less to your liking.'

'That's all you understand, isn't it?' she asked. 'The language of force.'

'Diamond, I have no wish to quarrel with you. I prefer to think of this as an aberration, best forgotten on both sides. I said that I would not forgive you, but I do, because I can't help myself. Let us put this behind us, and return to that world where we are one.'

'I don't think we can ever return to that world,' she said sadly. 'It didn't really exist.'

She wasn't sure when he'd moved towards her, but suddenly he seemed very close, dominating her by his sheer intense vitality. Fran tried to step back from him but she couldn't move. When he touched her she trembled.

'Don't,' she whispered. 'Don't...'

'Don't ask me not to touch you, when touching you is all my joy. Don't ask me to believe there is no joy for you in my touch.'

'I have never denied it,' she said huskily. 'But there has to be more...or there is nothing...'

He silenced her by laying his fingers lightly on her lips. The touch burned her. She turned her head away but he laid his lips against her neck.

'There is this,' he murmured, his breath scorching her.

She tried to protest but the sensation aroused beautiful memories, and she had to fight not to succumb to them.

'Ali—no,' she pleaded. 'There's so much still to say—'

'But we are saying it,' he murmured, lifting her and carrying her to the bed.

He undressed her and himself quickly. Fran tried to fight her own sensations, but her body had changed since yesterday. Now it was a body that had known him in the bittersweet intimacy of passion. It had responded to him as to no other man, and as it never would again. It flowered for him. It loved him.

Her mind might be full of anger and despair, but his caresses made her want to weep tears of happiness. And he seemed to know it, and used his knowledge shamelessly to make her acknowledge him as her king, as she never would do in words.

When he began to kiss her breasts she arched helplessly against him, seeking the skilful movements of his tongue. As she felt him give what she craved the heat seemed to rise up and engulf her, melting resistance.

His hands caressed her everywhere, finding her intimately before he moved over her to claim her deeply. At the moment of union she sighed, and even she could not have said whether it was a sound of joy or anguish. She loved him so much, and she'd discovered her love in such heart-rending circumstances.

When he had left her, he did not turn away, but held her close, prolonging the intimacy of loving.

'You see,' he whispered, 'how it can be with us— how it must always be; you must never leave me— you belong to me.'

At the word 'belong' her mouth tried to shape the word 'no', but only silently. And what use was a word against the burning, joyful affirmation of her flesh.

He continued to hold her warmly, until the heat and the physical contentment overcame her and she slept in his arms. But even in sleep she was troubled. Ali's loving had been beautiful, ecstatic, but she knew in her heart that it had also been another assertion of his power. He had demonstrated that he could subdue her, not through his desire, but through her own. She was as much a prisoner as ever.

When she awoke he was still there, regarding her tenderly.

'I told you once that I would only be satisfied when you yielded to me completely, in your heart as well as your body,' he reminded her. 'When you said that you were mine for all time and desired only to remain with me. Say it, Diamond. Let me hear you say the words, and swear that they are true.'

She looked up at him from the pillow in despair.

'I will never say those words, Ali.'

She wept as she spoke, because her heart told her that it was true. She loved him beyond reason, loved him so much that she was engulfed by him. But she must resist her love and never, ever admit it to him.

He scowled as he heard her. He could see the glisten of her tears, and they caused an unfamiliar pain in his breast. But that was something he must conceal.

He rose, and turned away from the bed, hiding from her. Her power over him must be resisted and never acknowledged, lest she unman him. He had threatened her with his wrath, but then forgiven her. She would despise him, because no woman respected a man who allowed her to rule him.

There was a noise in the outer tent. Swiftly Ali pulled a robe about him and went out. Fran heard muttered voices. Then Ali's voice rose in command. A moment later he was back with her.

'We are returning to the city,' he said. 'There is a message to say that my mother is on her way home. I would like to be there before her, to show my respect.'

'Where has she been?'

'In New York. Hurry now.'

The flight back over the desert at night was magical. Far below them lights gleamed out of the velvety blackness. Gradually they went lower and lower, until the landing on the palace roof. Fran was escorted back to her apartment by a guard of honour that had mysteriously doubled in size since last time.

Ali's secretary greeted him with the news that Princess Elise had already arrived. He went straight to her apartments.

The princess was an elegant woman with snowy white hair and a beautiful, fine-boned face. She had been born in London, sixty years ago, but now she looked every inch eastern royalty. She rose and greeted Ali with open arms, and a brilliant smile that made her face young again.

'My son!' she said warmly.

He hugged her with enthusiasm. 'You look younger every time I see you. Did you enjoy your trip?'

'Yes, it was very satisfactory. You will find the fruit of my work in there.' She made a gesture towards a desk on which several files lay. 'I hope you'll approve of what I have done.'

'When have I ever questioned any decision of yours? Put business aside for the moment and let me look at you.'

He stood back, holding her at arm's length until he was satisfied. Then he grinned and hugged her again.

'You look remarkably well for a woman who's just flown all the way from New York,' he observed.

'Actually, I took a little detour to London. I seem to have arrived just after you left. And while I was there I heard some strange stories about you.'

He laughed and settled himself on the sofa, accepting the drink she offered him. 'People talk. When have I ever worried about that?'

'Perhaps you should have worried a little more. The servants in your house didn't know how to answer my questions. They shuffled their feet and tried to get away, until I had to be very firm. Now tell me about this English girl that you have "invited" to be your guest.'

Ali shrugged in a light-hearted way, but actually he was as uneasy as his own steward under his mother's piercing gaze. Here was one woman who saw through him and would tolerate nothing less than honesty, which made her uncomfortably like another woman, at this minute in his palace.

'Miss Frances Callam is enjoying my hospitality for a while,' he said. 'Tell me more about your trip.'

'All in good time, my son. I've had to play private detective to find my way through a garbled story about an employment agency, and a servant girl who vanished when you did. Through the agency I found myself talking to an enquiry agent called Joey, who is concerned because he cannot contact Miss Callam. I reassured him, hoping that I was right to do so.'

'Quite right, Mother. Miss Callam is in no danger.'

'Ali, why can't you meet my eye?'

'Believe me, Mother, you are making a fuss about nothing.' Elise was looking at him wryly, and he reddened under that all-seeing gaze.

'Ali, there are some laws that even you cannot ignore. I won't ask what you've done, because it might be better for me not to know. But I expect you to bring this young woman to meet me tomorrow.'

'Yes, Mother,' he said meekly.

CHAPTER TEN

ELISE'S apartment was a clever combination of royal luxury and English comfort. She was immediately above Fran's own rooms, looking out onto the Peacock Garden, and her sitting room was filled with light. Long net curtains filled the floor-length windows and wafted gently in the faint breeze.

She rose, a tall, graceful figure in white robes, and embraced Fran warmly.

'I have longed for this meeting,' she said, adding mysteriously, 'I've heard so much about you that it has made me most curious.'

Tea was served. It was good, solid English tea, because, as Elise explained, 'After thirty-five years in this country I still can't do without my cuppa.'

'Oh, yes,' Fran said, sipping gratefully.

They made polite small talk, with occasional interjections from Ali, until Elise said with a touch of exasperation, 'My son, I'm sure you have affairs of state to attend to.'

'No today,' he said, smiling at them both. 'If I leave you may talk about me.'

'Certainly we are going to talk about you. Please go away at once. Can't you see when you are not wanted?'

He gave a wry glance first to his mother, then Fran, before reluctantly leaving.

When they were alone Elise kissed Fran on both cheeks and smiled.

'I knew you would be beautiful,' she said, 'from the effect you have had on my son. But you are more than beautiful. Speak to me quite frankly, I beg you. Are you here of your own free will?'

'No,' Fran said, and Elise's face darkened.

'We will talk of that later,' she said heavily. 'For now, tell me how you met.'

Fran described the first evening, and what had happened subsequently. When she came to the part about the cheque, Elise said, 'Ah! Now I understand something that has been puzzling me. Come with me.'

She took Fran's hand and led her into the next room. Fran stopped dead on the threshold. This room didn't belong to a female forced to live in retirement. This was a business office, complete with desks, filing cabinets and all the latest equipment.

Two young women were busy at computers. They rose and bowed when the princess entered, and she waved them lightly away. Under Fran's astonished eye she went to a third computer and began to tap in some figures. A file opened on the screen and Elise beckoned her to look.

'Normally Ali gives the ICF one million a year,' Elise observed calmly. 'When he suddenly added another hundred thousand I couldn't understand it. He never does such things without first consulting me.'

'A million?' Fran echoed in dismay. 'And—consulting you?'

'I handle all his donations to foreign charities.'

'All his—?'

'About twenty million a year.' Elise gave her lovely smile again. 'My dear, have you fallen for the legend of the playboy who spends every penny on himself? How unwise of you!

'Ali maintains this grandiose palace because it's expected of him, but the oil revenues are spent first on his subjects, and only afterwards on himself. I must show you some of our hospitals. They are simply the best equipped in the world.'

'But why didn't he tell me this instead of just saying loftily that he wouldn't discuss it?' Fran said in frustration.

'Because he is a prince,' Elise said, amused. 'He doesn't feel he has to explain himself to anybody. You take him on his terms or not at all.'

'And all those things he told me about not discussing serious things with women—' Fran said with mounting indignation.

'He was probably trying to annoy you. And it's true that he wouldn't talk with a strange woman, nor does he appoint women to his cabinet. He makes an exception for me because I am his mother. In this country, a man who does not respect his mother is considered a disgrace.

'I remember years ago, in England, my own brother once quarrelling with our mother and telling her to shut up. No Kamari man would speak like that to the woman who gave him life.'

She gestured towards the computer.

'He takes his charities very seriously indeed, and they are all in my hands. If people wish to solicit donations they come to me, not to him. I visit them, and advise Ali according to what I discover. That is why I have been out of the country recently.'

'And I thought it was a shopping trip.'

'Well, I indulged myself with a little shopping as well.'

'I can't take all this in,' Fran said, dazed.

'Then I will give you some more.' Elise pressed a buzzer on her desk and spoke into an intercom. 'Be good enough to have my car brought around to the front.'

Ten minutes later the two women were seated in the back of the princess's personal limousine, gliding into the heart of town. They stopped outside a huge white-walled building, which Elise explained was the city hospital.

'We shall have to go through the private part first, but quickly.'

The private section was much like a private hospital anywhere, but it was the public wards that alerted Fran.

'These are for people who cannot afford to pay,' Elise explained. 'The money comes from state funds, or, in other words, Ali.'

Everywhere she looked Fran saw spotless cleanliness, the finest equipment and a high ratio of staff to patients. She had to admit that the place shamed a good many western hospitals.

'The people with money are charged heavily,' Elise said, 'and they partly pay for the poor patients. But only partly. The rest of the money comes from the royal coffers.'

'From the oil,' Fran mused.

'Not just from the oil. The casinos make a handsome profit.'

'Casinos? Plural?'

'In almost every capital city in the world, and several in Las Vegas. We need all the profit we can make because Ali has some very expensive ideas for irrigating the desert. So far most of the money has been soaked up by the sand, but he keeps trying one ex-

periment after another.' Elise smiled fondly. 'Sometimes there's a touch of the mad professor about my
son.'

She saw Fran craning her neck out of the window.
'Something interests you?'

'The Sahar Palace. Ali told me how it was built and
then abandoned as not being big enough.'

'Did he tell you what it's used for now?'

'No, I thought it was just standing empty.'

'And he let you think that,' Elise said with motherly
exasperation. She said something in Arabic to the
driver, and the car turned into the palace entrance.

As they went through the main gates the big front
door opened and two women came hurrying out, smiling as they saw their visitor. They were followed by
a stream of children who engulfed Elise, with scant
regard to her royalty.

'They all love it when Her Highness visits us,' one
of the women confided to Fran. 'They have no mothers
of their own, so in their hearts she is their mother.'

'This is an orphanage?' Fran asked.

'Of course,' Elise said. 'Ali insisted that this place
must be put to good use, and what better use can there
be than the future of our country? Come inside. I think
you will see things that will surprise you.'

But Fran was no longer surprised by any revelation.
The home clearly had a generous budget and was well
staffed and equipped, but it was the place's warm
atmosphere that delighted her. She had begun to realise that she knew nothing about Ali and the way he
ran his country.

At the rear of the orphanage were the classrooms.
Girls were taught apart from boys, but Fran's alert

eyes noted that their science equipment was equally good.

'My husband was an enlightened man,' Elise explained. 'Which is to say that he listened to me,' she added with a twinkle. 'I made him see the need for women to be properly educated. My son is the same. His ideas are old-fashioned, but the right woman could make him listen.'

She smiled, apparently not needing a reply to this, which was lucky because Fran was far from knowing what to say.

'Do the casinos pay for all this?' she asked, changing the subject.

'No, this is the London property portfolio.'

It wasn't until they returned to the palace that Elise demanded full details of Fran's presence in Kamar. She listened composedly, only a small furrow on her forehead betraying any sign of disturbance. When the story was finished she simply said, 'How charming.'

They had tea together, then Elise declared that she was tired and needed to lie down. But as soon as Fran had departed Elise picked up the phone and demanded, in a voice that promised trouble, to be connected to her son.

He arrived to find her pacing the floor, and her first words contained no welcome, and certainly no respect.

'My son, are you quite mad? This young woman is a writer for several internationally respected publications. She has friends in high places, and you have simply kidnapped her. Are you asking for an international incident?'

'There will be no incident that I can't smooth over,' Ali said arrogantly. 'They need our oil.'

'I like you least when you talk like that,' Elise snapped, and he had the grace to blush.

'You don't understand, Mother,' he said at last. 'Fran and I—understand each other. We have done so from the first moment when I met her in the casino.' His eyes kindled. 'At least, so I thought. Later I discovered that she went there on purpose to find out about me.'

'And so you fell in love with her and took her home,' Elise said wryly.

'Certainly not. I took her home but there was no question of falling in love. She was a pleasant companion for a night.'

'Really,' Elise said with a touch of scorn. 'Continue. I am agog!'

'When we talked—something changed. Her mind enchanted me. She took me back to my childhood, and the magic stories I loved to read. She knew them too. I could talk to her. We felt so close, but she wouldn't tell me her name.

'Then I was summoned away, on business, and when I returned she had gone.'

Elise's lips twitched. 'She just walked out on you?'

'Yes!' Ali's voice had an edge. 'But she returned two days later, as herself. I'd agreed to see a journalist; I was expecting a man. Naturally I refused to talk to her.'

'Naturally,' Elise murmured.

'While I was away, she gained entry to my house, pretending to be a maid.'

'And so you decided to teach her a lesson. For what, I wonder? For her methods, or for daring to reject you?'

Ali flung her a dark look, but made no comment.

'So,' Elise continued thoughtfully, 'if you're not afraid of an international incident, it seems that all you have to worry about is Mr Howard Marks.'

'Who is he? I've never heard of him.'

'I gather he is Miss Callam's fiancé.'

'Impossible,' Ali said at once. 'If that were true she would never have——' He stopped. His mother was looking at him with eyes raised. 'Never mind.'

'Perhaps I should have spoken of this last night, but first I wanted to meet this young woman, and see what kind of person she is. Now I think I know. Mr Marks is a banker. He has been going out with Miss Callam for some time, and has it in mind to marry her. He is evidently an extremely good match. Of course, I've been out of England for some time, but in my day a good match was the kind of thing a girl had to think of very seriously.'

'Then why did she never speak to me of this man?'

'From what I can see, you haven't given her much chance to tell you anything.'

'Then she can tell me now,' Ali said grimly, rising to his feet.

Fran was lying down with her hands clasped behind her head, brooding on what she had learned that day. Her picture of Ali as a self-indulgent playboy had been wrong all the time. That was merely what he allowed the world to think. Behind the scenes he was a true father to his people. She felt happiness stealing over her at being able to think the best of him.

She wondered when she would see him. He would probably want to devote some time to his mother, but later perhaps he might come to her. She was eager to see him in this new light, and to let him know how her heart had warmed to him.

At last she heard his footsteps outside, and sat up eagerly as he came into the room.

'Why didn't you tell me about—?' they both said together, and stopped.

'I've been talking with my mother,' Ali said. 'Why did you never speak to me of Howard Marks?'

For a moment Fran had to think who he meant. Howard and the life he represented was so far away.

'Ali—I don't understand—'

'Howard Marks—the man you were planning to marry. My mother knows all about him, so don't pretend that you don't. How could you have concealed such a thing from me?'

A moment ago she'd been full of tenderness towards him, but at this flash of the old, imperious Ali her temper rose quickly.

'How could I—? Well, you've got a nerve!' She bounded off the bed and confronted him. 'Don't tell me that my disappearance has been noticed after all?'

'Evidently. According to my mother, Mr Marks has been asking questions, claiming to be your future husband. This was something you should have told me.'

Fran stared at him, outraged beyond speech. She hadn't mentioned Howard because Ali had driven him right out of her mind. In Ali's arms no other man had existed. But there was no way she could say such a thing to this arrogant, overbearing man who barked out his unreasonable orders like a tyrant.

'You're very fond of telling people what they should do,' she seethed. 'Perhaps it's you that should listen. I never asked to come here; I was tricked into it. I don't recall you enquiring if there was a man in my life.'

'Are you saying that there is?'

'Are you saying it would have made a difference?'

They glared at each other, both furious.

'Was he the man with you at the casino?' he snapped.

'Of course not. That was Joey. I wouldn't take Howard on a job.'

'Ah, yes, you were on a job. A job entitled "the seduction of a prince". You naturally wouldn't want to tell Mr Marks about that.'

'There was nothing to tell. You may recall that there was no seduction—'

'Yes, you slipped out when my back was turned,' he said grimly.

'So you did know I'd gone,' she said triumphantly. 'That story of yours about not coming back was just to fool me.'

He regarded her coldly, and she guessed he was furious with himself for the slip.

'It seems we've both been playing a game of delusion,' he said at last, in a voice harsher than she'd ever heard him use before. 'You set out to trick me into thinking you were a true woman with a heart to offer, and you were very convincing, for a while.'

'Was it my heart you wanted, Ali? I wonder. Maybe we both played games at first, but we weren't playing for hearts.'

'Yes, I know the prize you were after,' he said grimly. 'Not a heart but a scoop for your paper. And I taught you that I'm not a man to be played with. Now tell me about this man who plans to marry you.

What kind of man is he who permits you to take such risks?'

'Howard doesn't permit or not permit. He understands that I'm my own woman, not subject to his orders.' Furious indignation made her say the next words. 'It will be a great relief to get back to him.'

Ali drew a sharp breath. 'Do you think I'm going to let you return to the west with the secrets you've discovered?'

'What secrets? I've learned about your charities, not your national security.'

He didn't answer in words, but he gave her a burning stare that told her his true meaning. Facts and figures weren't the only secrets. There were also the secrets of a man's heart that could be learned only in his arms, in his bed, when two eager bodies became one in the life of true passion. These were the secrets that lived in the night, in the incoherent words of love too deep to be spoken. They were secrets a man might turn away from by day because they confronted him with a self that he feared. But they couldn't be denied, and his eyes told her that he would kill them both before letting her expose them to a derisive world.

But how could he know her so little, she wondered wildly, as not to understand that he could trust her with these things, because for her too they were sacred?

'Even you must know by now that you can't keep me here for ever,' she said.

'But I can, and I will. My mother says that I have compromised you, and so deprived you of a good marriage. Very well. Then I have a duty towards you. I will replace a good marriage with a better one. As my wife you will have nothing to complain of.'

'Your wife?' she echoed, aghast.

'Our marriage will take place immediately.'

'Our marriage will never take place,' she flung at him. 'I won't stay with a man who informs me of our wedding as though he's doing me a favour.'

'You will stay,' Ali said, 'and you will become my wife. The truth that is between us will prevail and make our marriage a happy one. I shall give instructions immediately, and the ceremony will take place in three days' time.'

'It will not,' Fran cried wildly. 'Ali, understand once and for all that I won't marry you. Not in three days' time. Not ever.'

'My mind is made up. There is nothing further to discuss,' he said calmly, and walked out.

Marriage, for a ruler of Kamar, was a complex business. Officially it was a secular state. Three of the world's great religions lived peacefully side by side, with no one religion predominating.

So there would be, in effect, four weddings. The first was a civil ceremony, conducted in a small room in the palace. Then the ruler and his bride would present themselves at each of the three main religious headquarters in the city for the pronouncement of a blessing. These were riotous occasions, with the public thronging the entrances, clapping and cheering.

If this had been a normal wedding Fran would have enjoyed the buzz of preparation. From dawn to dusk she was engulfed in the making of a new wardrobe, and the selection of adornments for her state rooms. Instead, she floated through it all in an unhappy dream, wondering how she could be so miserable when her life was about to be joined to that of the man she loved. No, she amended that. The man she could have loved. For he seemed bent on destroying her feelings for him.

Elise had said the right woman could make Ali listen, but he showed no sign of listening. And in this tyranny Fran saw an ominous portent for their future.

Two days before the wedding Ali departed on a flying visit to the north of his little country, stating that he would return the following day. Elise came to spend the evening with her future daughter-in-law.

'You'll be glad to know that Yasir will not trouble you again,' she said. 'His wound is superficial and healing well, and he will have left the country before your wedding. Ali has banned him from returning in less than five years.'

'That's good,' Fran said.

Elise observed her critically. 'You don't look like a happy bride preparing for her big day.'

'Don't I?' Fran asked listlessly.

'Anyone would think you were going to your execution instead of your wedding.'

'Well, it feels like the end of my life.'

'How ungrateful you are! Ali will make you the princess of a wealthy country. You'll never have to lift a finger again.'

'Is that why you married?' Fran asked, regarding Elise levelly.

It fascinated her to observe that even now the mention of her late husband could bring a faint blush to Elise's cheek.

'I married the man I loved more than anything in life,' Elise said. 'And I knew that he loved me the same way.'

'You're lucky it was that easy for you,' Fran said wistfully.

Elise gave her rich laugh. 'It wasn't easy at all. We had terrible fights, especially in the first year. But we survived them all, because we knew that we couldn't bear to be apart. Whatever happened, we *knew* how much we loved and needed each other.'

She fell silent, leaving the implication hanging in the air. Fran met her eyes.

'Is that how you love my son?' Elise asked at last.

'I don't know,' Fran said desperately. 'How can I know when he's forcing me into this wedding? Because he knows his own feelings he thinks that's all that matters.'

'But what makes you think he knows his own feelings?' Elise asked.

'Well, he's certainly acting like a man who knows.'

'Nonsense. He's acting like a man in the depths of confusion. Does he really love you? Or does he only want you? Even he doesn't know. But he thinks if he acts firmly the confusion will sort itself out by magic. He's wrong, of course. He's merely ensuring that he'll never know the truth. And neither will you if this ridiculous marriage is allowed to go ahead.'

'I thought you approved of me,' Fran said.

'But I do. I think you're extremely good for him. You've got him not knowing whether he's coming or going, and he needs some uncertainty. He's had things all his own way for far too long. I want to see you married to Ali, but, oh, Fran, my dear—not like this.'

'Have you said all this to him?'

'Of course I have, and I might as well have been talking to a brick wall. The men of this family have always been distinguished for their stubbornness, and their inability to see beyond the ends of their noses. I'm sorry to say that my son is a chip off several unfortunate old blocks. Your sons will probably be the same.'

'You mean—my sons with Ali? Will they ever exist, I wonder?'

'They will if we act sensibly. You say you don't know how much you love Ali. But do you love him enough to leave him?'

A bleakness settled over Fran's heart. To leave him, perhaps for ever, never to ride beside him, never again to lie in his arms?

But the alternative was to live by his side as his chief concubine—for she would be little more than that—enjoying his desire but not his respect, never knowing the truth of his heart or her own, and seeing their love wither in that uncertainty.

'Yes,' she whispered. 'I love him enough for that.'

'In that case,' Elise said decisively, 'we have work to do.'

It was unlike the princess to act impulsively, but when she announced her immediate departure nobody dared to argue. Ali's chief adviser ventured to suggest that His Highness might prefer her to wait until his return, but she gave him her chilliest and most imperious stare until he faltered into silence. When he gathered his wits sufficiently to remind her that the wedding was set for two days hence, she informed him loftily, and with perfect truth, that she would have returned by then.

Instantly a smooth-running machine was set in motion. The princess's personal limousine was brought to the front to wait for her with its engine running. A message was sent to her state apartments and a moment later Her Highness emerged, accompanied by a heavily veiled maidservant. In a few minutes they were in the car, on their way to the airport, and the flight to London.

Another limousine was waiting at the other end, to take them to Ali's house. After a brief pause there, it set off again for the short journey to Fran's address, where it disgorged the 'maidservant', now without her Arab garb and veils. The whole business had taken under twelve hours.

CHAPTER ELEVEN

ELISE was back in Kamar by noon next day. Ali reached the palace an hour later. Within minutes he was on his way to his mother's room.

The thunder of his boots on the tiled floor caused a quaking everywhere, except in the princess's apartment. She sat calmly writing at her desk, waiting for her son to arrive. The slam of the door shook the building. She glanced up, then returned to what she was doing.

Ali cast a glowering look at her bent head, and set about pacing the floor. When he'd covered the ground several times he snapped, 'My grandfather would have fed you to the alligators for what you've done.'

'Your grandfather was an exceedingly foolish man,' Elise observed calmly. 'I regret to say that you seem to have inherited the worst of his foolishness. Of course I got her away. Whatever were you thinking of to let things get so far?'

'She is the bride I have chosen,' Ali growled.

'But has she chosen you? Marry her at the sword's point and you would never know.'

'Do you think I know nothing about her heart? There have been such things between us—I cannot tell even you—' He found himself reddening, and turned away from his mother's understanding eyes. 'I promise you, I know her heart.'

'No, my son, you know only her passion. Her heart is a secret to you. And when passion dies?'

'That will never happen.'

'For you, perhaps. But a woman's heart is different. For her, passion is nothing without love. How can she know that you love her when you have behaved with arrogance and unkindness, and treated her wishes as though they were nothing?'

'Everything I have is hers. What can she ask that it will not be my pleasure to give?'

'Her freedom. Freedom to choose you—or reject you.'

He paled. 'Reject me?'

'You must win her, so that she can choose you freely.'

'And if she does not?' he asked, almost inaudibly.

'Then you must let her go. Unless her happiness is more to you than your own, you do not truly love her, and she is right to refuse you.'

'You're asking me to beg from a woman.'

'If she's the woman I think her, she won't make you beg.'

'But to humble myself—to go to her as a suppliant, uncertain of her answer— I am the prince.'

'And have never had to ask for what you wanted. It's time you learned.'

'And if I can't?'

'Then she will never be yours,' Elise said simply.

He wheeled away from her sharply. His mother watched him with sympathy and pity. It was hard for her to do this to him. Only the knowledge that his eventual happiness depended on it had given her the courage.

When at last he spoke again his voice was shaking. 'I can't believe that she left without a message to me—not a single word.'

'Have you looked everywhere?'

He stared at her, and after a moment he hurried out of the room.

The maids were still in Fran's apartment. They took one look at his face and scattered. Ali raged through the rooms, looking for he knew not what. Somewhere, surely, there must be a sign that she hadn't simply turned her back on him. Because if she had done that then everything he'd thought was between them was no more than a mockery.

At last he found what he was looking for on a little inlaid table, held down by a gold box. He opened out the single sheet of paper and read:

My Darling,

I know you'll think it's a terrible betrayal, my leaving you, but try to understand that I have no choice. Nobody should get married like this. There would never be peace between us, and eventually there would be nothing at all.

Do you remember my dream of a flying carpet? Well, it happened, as you meant it to. The magician cast his spells and the prince came out of the coloured smoke. He was handsome and charming, and he showed me wonders that will live in my heart for ever.

It was a lovely dream and I shall always remember that I once had a little magic, all my own. But, sadly, magic doesn't last, and the carpet flies away again.

Goodbye, my darling. I wonder where we'll meet again? Will it be in the Enchanted Gardens? Were we ever destined to find them? Or maybe they don't really exist.

I've wondered how to sign this letter. You gave me so many names, and it was lovely pretending to be them for a while. But they were only illusions, and I can't live on illusions. If you can't love the woman I really am, let us forget each other.

No, not forget. Never. But put the dream aside as too beautiful to be true. I've signed this letter with the one name you never called me, but the only one that was true. Try to forgive me.

The letter was signed, 'Frances.'

When he'd finished reading Ali realised how quiet and empty the apartment was. Where once there had been her laughter, now there was nothing. Her defiance had enraged him, but he would have given all he had to have her there again, telling him that she would do as she pleased, no matter what he thought. With what courage she had opposed him, and how wonderful that courage seemed now.

Only the soft plashing of the fountains broke the silence, and suddenly he realised that another noise was missing. He'd grown used to the cooing of her white doves, the faithful birds that would never leave her. He strode out to the courtyard.

But the dovecote was empty. The doves had flown away.

He knew then that she had really gone.

It was strange, Fran thought, how you could love a man so much that it hurt. You could dream of him at night and yearn for him by day. The memory of his passion and your own could make your flesh ache with longing. He could fill your heart and thoughts until nothing else existed in the whole world.

And yet you could force yourself to leave him, and know that you'd done the right thing. You could struggle not to be crushed by your own heartbreak and resist the fierce temptation to run back to him.

For the first few days she flinched whenever the telephone rang, certain that it must be Ali. But it never was. She'd half expected an explosion of wrath at her defection. But perhaps he would simply ask her to talk, say that he understood, and wanted to start again, without coercion. If he truly loved her...

But there were no telegrams or letters, and nobody came to the door. It was as though he had wiped her out of his existence, and a shiver went through her. He'd planned to marry her out of duty, because he'd 'compromised' her. Her departure had actually been a relief to him, and now it was all over.

Barney, a kindly elderly man who ran *The Financial Review*, threw up his hands at the sight of her.

'So the prodigal returns! There was a crazy rumour that you were going to marry Prince Ali.'

'Crazy,' Fran agreed with her brightest smile. 'You shouldn't believe all you hear. But I have been in Kamar.'

'Great! So what really happens to all that money?'

'He spends it on his people.'

'Oh, c'mon; the story must be better than that.'

'It's the truth. He doesn't make a big fuss about it because he thinks it's nobody else's business. But he isn't the way we thought. In fact, I don't think there's a story there at all.'

The editor's jaw dropped. 'No story?'

'Well, if there is, I can't write it. I'm sorry.'

'Then I'll have to assign someone else.'

'I wish them luck,' Fran said with a wan little smile.

Once she would have thought herself crazy to give up an assignment, but what had happened to her was something that could never be mined as raw material for a feature. It was too precious, too sacred.

Howard called. After the volcanic emotions of the last few weeks his kindly, slightly pompous voice sounded very welcome, and she agreed to have dinner with him.

Luckily he was a man of little imagination, and he readily accepted the story that she had been in Kamar to work.

'You really have been the mystery woman,' he said, when he'd ordered an excellent supper at an expensive restaurant. Howard always ate at expensive restaurants. He felt it was expected of a man in his position. 'You might have given me a call, my dear.'

'I'm sorry, Howard, there was a lot going on.'

'Of course, of course. And I've been very busy myself. There's a bit of manoeuvring going on at the bank. The chief executive is retiring, and—er—' he coughed modestly '—it's between me and one other fellow.'

'I'm sure the other fellow doesn't have a chance,' Fran said dutifully.

'Well, if I could bring some spectacular new business it would certainly help.' He smiled at her. 'I've missed you, my dear. I enjoy taking you to dinner. You're a fine-looking woman, and you make me very proud.'

'Your hair...is like a river of molten gold... How your eyes enthral me!'

Fran closed her eyes against the sound of Ali's voice whispering passionate hymns to her beauty. When would those memories cease to torment her?

'Well,' Howard said, filling her wine glass, 'I hope it was all worth it.'

'Worth it?'

'I mean did you gather plenty of material?'

'Well—'

'You must brief me about Kamar. It's a big nut and I'd like to crack it. That would really be a feather in my cap.'

Fran repeated what she'd told the editor about how Ali handled the Kamari budget, and his lavish giving to charity. Howard listened with a gleam in his eye that told her he was mentally taking notes.

It was a dull evening because Howard was a dull man, but dullness was what she wanted right now. It relaxed her tortured nerves, even though nothing was going to ease the pain in her heart. He drove her home and gave her a brief kiss goodnight, but she escaped before it could develop into anything more intense.

She had been home a week when she received an excited call from Barney.

'I've just had a call from Prince Ali's office. We can do the feature with his co-operation, the lot.'

'That's wonderful, Barney. I'm very pleased for you.'

'Not me, love, you.'

'I've told you, I can't do it.'

'You have to. Prince Ali made it a condition. You or nobody.'

At the words 'You have to,' something inside Fran flinched. This was the old Ali, laying down the law, insisting on his own way, giving her no choice. He wanted to see her again, but it was beneath his dignity to ask, so he tried to coerce her. He'd learned nothing.

'It can't be me,' she said in a tense voice.

'Fran, if you turn down a scoop like this I'll have to say you're unreliable, and then I couldn't use you again.'

'All right,' Fran said in a smouldering voice, 'I'll do it.'

Even now the signs of Ali's power were all around her. She arrived home to discover that some files, containing a wealth of material about Kamar, had been delivered in her absence.

There was also a typewritten note, saying that she would be given twenty-four hours to master the material, and then Ali's secretary would see her.

Perhaps that meant he wouldn't be there himself. This was a farewell gift. Afterwards she would hear of him no more, and somehow she would try to persuade herself that it was for the best.

Reading the file, she felt as though somebody had let her into Aladdin's cave. All the doors she had knocked on fruitlessly were now open to her. With what she had learned while in Kamar, she had the basis for a splendid feature. Once that would have been enough.

She made a long list of questions, and on the appointed day she approached Ali's house. The huge front door opened while she was still halfway up the path.

Ali's secretary advanced to meet her with a bow. If he knew that this was the woman who'd jilted his master he gave no sign of it.

'His Highness regrets profoundly that he is unable to be present. He has instructed me to give you all the help you require.'

So she wouldn't see Ali. When her heart had recovered from its pang of disappointment she would feel relieved.

Everything was ready for her. Ali's secretary was prepared with answers to all her questions. At her request he opened computer files and explained everything with perfect courtesy. Finally, he said, 'I'll arrange for some tea to be served to you.'

He slipped quietly out, leaving Fran frowning at the screen, concentrating too hard to hear a movement in the room.

'I hope everything is to your liking.'

She looked up quickly to see Ali watching her, and now she realised that she'd always secretly known that he would be there.

'Your secretary told me you were away,' she said.

'I instructed him to say that. I was afraid that otherwise you would leave.'

'Still manipulating people,' she observed.

He gave a wry, mirthless smile. 'Well, I'm afraid the habit is ingrained by now.'

'That's what I was afraid of. I tried to tell you in my letter—'

'Yes, your letter. Let's not discuss that.'

'No, let's discuss why you pulled so many strings to get me here. Or is that simply what I should have expected of you?'

'I don't understand your attitude,' he said in a hard voice. 'You made a fool of me before my people. In return I'm giving you what you wanted.'

'Giving? Or commanding? You told my editor it had to be me and nobody else.'

'It didn't occur to me that you would refuse. I wanted to see you, to give you a chance to explain your behaviour.'

'Explain? You kidnapped me and I escaped. What is there to explain?'

'I offered you honourable marriage—'

'You didn't offer me, you ordered me, just as you're ordering now. I refused but you wouldn't listen.'

'Because I couldn't understand how you could prefer your cold-blooded Englishman—'

'He looks cold-blooded to you because he knows how to behave with some restraint. He doesn't just grab anything he wants. He respects me.'

'Respects!' Ali said scornfully. 'I despise his kind of respect which is nothing but another name for cowardice. He respects you so much that it was days before he knew you were missing.'

'Because Howard doesn't demand an account of every moment of my life. He doesn't treat me like a possession.'

'Oh, you westerners! You know nothing. "People aren't possessions", "People don't own each other", "You can't belong to someone else". You see, I know all the standard phrases. But I come from a hot country, with hot-blooded people, and I tell you that if a man really loves a woman he wants her to belong to him in every possible way.

'It's not liberal, it's not fashionable, it's not correct, but if the love is there he wants everything about her— her heart, her mind, her body, her soul. He wants her thoughts to be of him, her heart to beat for him, and her passion to throb only for him. When she bears children, they must be his children.

'If she betrays his love his heart breaks. If he turns to find her, and she is not there, he doesn't wait days and then ask a few mild questions. He goes insane.'

She could almost believe that he had gone insane

that moment. His eyes burned with a fierce light and seemed to see right through her.

'Do you understand?' he grated. 'Do you know what you have done?'

'Yes, I left you,' she said breathlessly. 'It was what I had to do. I hoped that I could make you understand, but you can't understand, can you?'

'I understand that you belong with me, and this nonsense has to stop—'

'Stop saying "belong",' she insisted desperately. 'I don't belong to you. I never will. I can't love that way.'

'What is your way of loving?' he asked savagely. 'To drive a man to distraction and then abandon him, laugh at him?'

'I didn't—'

'Do you enjoy showing your power? Is that why you did this?'

'If you think that, we'll never understand each other,' she said desperately.

'Talk!' he said contemptuously. 'All this is talk.' He seized her and tried to pull her into his arms. 'Come back with me, and I will make you the most envied woman in Kamar. We can forget this and all shall be well between us again. Come back with me, Diamond—'

'Don't call me that,' she cried. 'Diamond never really existed. She cared for nothing but jewels and having people bow to her. She enjoyed being known as your favourite, and she didn't mind that it wasn't going to last, as long as she had her moment of triumph.

'But that's not me. My name is Frances and I don't like being piled high with jewels. They could be made of plastic for all I care. You wanted Diamond, but you

weren't interested in Frances. Ali, have you any idea
how wretched we would have made each other?'

It was as though she had struck him. He let his
hands fall and stepped back from her.

'You mean how wretched I would have made you,'
he said in a shocked voice.

'Yes,' she said sadly. 'I think you would. And I'd
have had to live with that wretchedness all my life.
But you could have consoled yourself with a succes-
sion of favourites.'

His eyes were murderous.

'You should not have said that to me.' He wheeled
away from her and began to stride the room. 'You
shouldn't have said it, but perhaps it's as well you did.
It shows how far apart we are. There would have been
no other woman but you, no other wife, no favourites.
That was how my father treated my mother, and how
I would have treated you.

'Have you forgotten the day I found my cousin
bleeding and you standing over him with a knife in
your hand? I arrested him because I knew that, how-
ever it looked, you must be innocent. That was how
much I trusted you. That was how close I thought we
were. If you never understood that, then truly our
minds never met.'

'No,' Fran said, nodding. 'That's exactly it. Our
minds never met.'

'And this banker—your mind meets his? Of course
you are half a banker yourself.'

'Luckily for you. How much did a mere woman
save you, Ali?'

'A great deal. I admitted that at the time and
thanked you. But I missed the real point—that you

have more in common with him than with me. You always did have, and you always will.'

He regarded her strangely. 'My mother was right, as she is about all things. He is a good marriage for you.'

'He's a good banker, if that's what you mean,' Fran said stiffly. 'Henderson & Carver is one of the most highly regarded merchant banks in London, and any day now he'll be appointed chief executive.'

It felt strange to hear herself talking in that stiff, 'proper' way when her heart was breaking at the distance that increased every moment between herself and the man she loved. But she couldn't bridge that distance, and only pride was left to sustain her.

There were lines of suffering etched on Ali's face, yet the words that came out belied that suffering. She had hurt him, and that hurt her, yet he would deny his own pain to her, and so keep her at a distance. And that was a denial of love.

'Chief executive,' Ali mused. 'What can I say to the woman who will be the wife of such a powerful man?'

'Don't jeer at me. I know he isn't as powerful as you—'

'He is nothing like me at all. And that's why you've chosen him, isn't it?'

'What's the point of talking about it?' she said wearily. 'Maybe I will marry Howard, maybe I won't—'

'Don't tell me he's hesitating?' Ali's face darkened and he turned away quickly. 'He's a fool,' he said over his shoulder.

'No, just a very cautious man.'

'If he was a clever man he would seize you while he had the chance.'

'Exactly,' she said in despair. 'Seize. That will always be the way you think.'

Suddenly she realised what a dangerous thing she'd done in coming here. This was Ali's territory, where she could simply be taken prisoner again.

At that moment he turned and their eyes met. With a gasp Fran seized up her bag, ran for the door, pulled it open and hurried out into the hall.

The doorman on duty was the same one as last time. He'd learned his lesson by now, and stood in front of the front door, arms folded.

Ali came out behind her. Fran turned to look at him with a face full of accusation.

'Let her go,' he said.

The porter stared, not sure he'd heard properly.

'*Let her go!*'

The door opened, and the next moment Fran was gone.

CHAPTER TWELVE

THE buzzer went on Howard Marks's desk. 'Someone to see you, Mr Marks,' came his secretary's voice.

'You must forgive my arriving without an appointment,' said the man in the doorway. 'But my business is rather urgent.'

'Your Highness,' Howard said, rising hastily to his feet. 'This is an unexpected honour.'

Ali regarded him askance. A voice was running through his head, making an ironic commentary on what was happening. It was unnerving because it was unfamiliar. In fact, it had never happened before he met Fran.

But the voice was there now, observing coolly, *After the rumours this man has heard he should be wanting to sock me on the jaw, not declaring my company to be an honour.*

But his smile gave no sign of this as he approached Howard's desk and began to unload his briefcase.

'Recent disturbing events have compelled me to make alterations in my financial arrangements,' he said smoothly. 'Men that I thought I could trust have turned out to be thieves. For this revelation I am greatly indebted to Miss Frances Callam, whose visit to my country has been most beneficial.'

'I had heard that she'd been to Kamar,' Howard said cautiously.

Ask me about it, damn you! said the voice. *Threaten*

*to break my neck if I laid a finger on her, as I would
do with you.*

When Howard said nothing Ali continued, 'She persuaded me to break my normal rule and give her unprecedented access for her feature. I am now very glad
that I did so. I have learned to trust her judgement.'

'I have always admired Miss Callam's business
sense,' Howard said gravely.

'It was her recommendation that persuaded me to
seek you out and suggest that you take on some of
Kamar's business.'

'Indeed!' Howard said.

*Oh, Diamond, if you could see this man's face now!
At the mention of business his eyes light up as they
never did at the sound of your name.*

For an hour they went through papers together.
When they had finished Ali said casually, 'Miss
Callam informs me that you are in line to become
chief executive.'

'It should be a certainty now,' Howard observed
with a grin, looking at the papers.

'I hope so,' Ali said formally. 'It would please me
to help to promote your marriage with Miss Callam,
which I understand is imminent.'

'Did she say so?' Howard asked eagerly.

'She spoke of you in the highest possible terms.'

'I say! By Jove! Really? Always a bit hard to know
what's going on in Fran's mind. She keeps her secrets,
you know.'

'Not from you, I feel sure,' Ali said. 'But I am em-
boldened to touch on a delicate matter, so that there
may be no misunderstandings. I hope your mind is
entirely without suspicion regarding Miss Callam. Her
visit to my country was made solely in pursuit of her

feature. She never forgot what was due to you, and she was treated at all times with respect.'

In saying this Ali was not conscious of uttering a falsehood. Respect had always been a part of his feelings for Fran, and it was when she had lain in his arms in the throes of passion that his respect for her had been deepest.

'Well, naturally,' Howard said, with an awkward laugh. 'I never imagined anything else.'

Then you should have done. If such a beautiful woman were mine—as I once dreamed she was—I would suffer torments at the thought of her under the eyes of men.

Aloud Ali said, 'Then all is well. I look forward to hearing of your marriage. I return to Kamar tonight, and you will be hearing from me soon.'

He inclined his head and left the room. Howard stared at the door for a moment, puzzled. At last he muttered, 'Funny fellow!'

Fran's flat was tiny by the side of her palatial apartment in Kamar, but now it felt like a refuge, and she loved it. It was on the ground floor, with French windows that opened onto a garden. On summer evenings she could sit with them open, looking out at the garden and listening to soft music.

That was what she was doing when Howard phoned her. But as she listened to what he had to say her relaxed mood was shattered.

'He actually came to see you?' she asked, dazed.

'You should see the business he's putting my way. Every bank in the world is after Kamari money and this should just about clinch it for me getting the job.'

He droned on about the job for a few minutes. Fran

listened on automatic, trying to take in this astonishing new development.

'You seem to have made a big impression on him,' Howard said. 'I didn't follow everything but I gather this has something to do with you.'

'I helped to show that he was being defrauded,' Fran said, through stiff lips.

'That's it. When he talked about us handling some of his affairs, he almost made it sound like he was giving you a dowry.'

'A—dowry?'

'Yes, he said he hoped we'd be happy and all that. He seemed to think your reputation had been compromised, and he wanted to make sure I hadn't misunderstood. Good of him, wasn't it?'

'Very good,' Fran whispered.

'So, all that remains now is to set the date. Why don't we have lunch tomorrow?'

She answered mechanically and hung up as soon as she could.

It was over, and now she knew the truth. Ali had acted out of possessiveness, not love, and he was probably glad to be rid of her. He was certainly acting like a man who wanted to draw a line under the whole business. She had been right to leave him.

But the ache of regret in her heart, for what might have been, couldn't be stilled.

It was getting late, and the light in the garden was beginning to fade. Fran switched on a small lamp and went to close the curtains. Then she started back with a gasp.

'I came to say goodbye,' Ali said.

'You—'

'Forgive me for not coming to the front door. I preferred to be discreet, having already caused you so much trouble. I also wanted to return these.'

He held out the files she'd left behind when she'd fled his house.

'Thank you,' she said blankly.

An awkward silence fell. This was the last time she would ever see him, and she didn't know what to say.

'Howard called me,' she said at last.

'Good. So now all is well.'

'Is it?'

'I finally understood what you'd been trying to tell me all this time. I thought I could give you everything, but all you wanted was to be free of me, and I wouldn't see it. I can love you best by letting you go. So let this be the end.'

'The end?' she whispered.

'I shall never trouble you again; you have my word on that. That's why I had to seek this last meeting, and tell you what was in my heart. From you I have learned many things: that love is more than passion, and the freedom of the heart is beyond price. It is over, Scheherazade. And you have won.'

'Don't call me that,' she cried, her eyes stinging with tears. She turned away so that he shouldn't see.

'It is how I shall always think of you, what I shall always call you in my heart. My Scheherazade, who set all my power at nothing, and outwitted me in the end. You have defeated me. Go in peace. Remember me kindly if you can. Forget me if you will. You, I shall never forget.'

She drew a deep shuddering breath at a strange note she heard in his voice, something that had never been there before. She forced herself to turn and face him.

But there was nobody there, only the curtains waving gently in the breeze.

On the flight home to Kamar, the prince sat in heavy silence, and nobody dared to approach him. When they landed he got into the back of the car without speaking, and was conveyed quickly to the palace.

'You did right, my son,' Elise said when she heard the whole story. 'Doubtless this is the best thing for her.'

'Will she be happy, Mother?'

'How can I tell? Was she happy with you?'

'I thought so—sometimes. But I was deluding myself. I saw what I wanted to see. I thought because I wanted her she must want me. I am wiser now.'

He spoke with a calm simplicity that might have fooled a casual onlooker. But Elise was not fooled. She saw the wretchedness in his eyes, heard the despair in his voice, and knew that this was a man whose life had ended.

'I am feeling a little tired,' she said with a sigh.

Instantly he was beside her. 'Have you seen the doctor?'

'Goodness, no. I'm not ill, merely tired.'

'You must take care of yourself, Mother.' He gave a wan smile. 'You are all I have now.'

'And it's time that was changed. You have gone too long without an heir, and we should be thinking of your marriage.'

He started back. 'How can you—when you know—?'

'I spoke of marriage, not of love. Your heart concerns only yourself. Your marriage concerns your country.'

'You are right. Select a bride for me, and present her to me on our wedding day. Since I can't marry the one my heart chooses, what does it matter who it is?'

He dropped on one knee beside her chair. 'Pity the woman who marries me, Mother. She will get a wretched bargain—a hollow man with no heart to give.'

'Time may change your feelings,' she said, stroking his face.

But Ali shook his head. 'Time will not change me. But I shall try to do my duty.'

'Well, do another duty for your mother. Take me to Wadi Sita. It's a while since I was there, and I should like to remember the old days, when you were a little boy, and we went there with your father.'

'I remember those days too. They were very happy. Life was simpler then. When do you wish to go?'

'Tomorrow, I think.'

Next day they boarded the helicopter and set out for Wadi Sita, landing in the darkness of early evening. Elise went to her tent and Ali joined her for supper an hour later. She had personally overseen the arrangements, and everything was laid out to please him. All his favourite foods were offered, and he smiled and thanked her. Yet the servants who moved silently in and out noticed that His Highness was abstracted, and ate without knowing.

A young man appeared, bearing a lyre. He bowed low, sat cross-legged on the carpet and began to sing.

'My heart rides with the wild wind...'

Ali tensed as he heard the bittersweet notes of the song that he'd once listened to with his beloved. But then he realised that Elise could not have known that, and it would be an insult to her to silence the singer. He sat with his head bent, trying not to hear the words that brought back so many tormenting memories.

> 'My steed is fast,
> My love rides by my side.'

She had ridden by his side in reality, as she still rode through his dreams, her hair tossed by the breeze, her eyes alight with something he had once dreamed was love.

But then she had ridden away from him, into the arms of a dullard. She had failed in courage at the last, but for that Ali blamed himself. It was he, with his selfishness, who had frightened her away. Everything might have been different, if only he had been different. That was the greatest pain of all.

The singer had reached the climax of the song. He had a powerful yet poignant voice, and he made it full of emotion.

> 'The wind is eternal,
> The sand is eternal.
> Our love is eternal.
> She is gone from me,
> But in my heart,
> We shall ride
> In the moonlight,
> For ever.'

Ali bent his head so that nobody might see his suffering. He had forced himself to make the sacrifice, but he had not yet taught himself to endure the thought of life without the one woman who gave life meaning.

As the song ended he muttered, 'Forgive me,' to his mother, and strode out of the tent as if pursued by furies.

His feet seemed to find their own way to the place where they had stood together beneath the palm tress, looking out over the desert. As ill luck would have it there was a full moon tonight, as brilliant and beautiful as before. But now *she* was gone, and he saw only the moon's coldness.

After a moment Elise came to stand beside him.

'I'm sorry, Mother,' he said. 'It was a mistake for me to come here, where she was.'

'Perhaps you were wrong to give her up so easily,' Elise suggested. 'You could still return to England, overwhelm her.'

He shook his head. 'No, that isn't the way.'

'Do you doubt your ability to make her say yes?'

'I doubt my will to do so. I could never again want to make her do anything. She must come to me willingly, or not at all. And now that can never be.'

He didn't see his mother's smile of satisfaction. She said, 'Then what will you do now?'

'Live as befits the man who loves her, and who has learned from her. It will not have been in vain. She taught me things that will always be part of me, and others will benefit.'

'Good, my son. That is how it should be. Let us now retire to bed. In your tent you will find a gift from me.'

'A gift?' He smiled. 'Your gifts were always the best. You thought of things that nobody else would think of. What is it?'

'Go and see. But remember, it is a very special gift.'

Frowning and puzzled, Ali turned and strode off to his tent. He went straight in, too preoccupied to notice that two white doves had come to rest immediately over the entrance.

The light was dim, only one small lamp burned, and at first he was unsure where to look. But then he discerned the tall, elegant figure of a woman, and his heart sank. How could his mother have done this? Did she think him so fickle that he could forget the love of his life in the arms of a stranger?

The young woman turned at his entrance and inclined her head gracefully towards him. She was heavily veiled. Ali stopped a few feet away from her.

'My lord,' she murmured.

He was too troubled in his mind to wonder that she spoke in English, but he automatically replied in the same language.

'Did my mother send you here?'

'Yes, my lord,' the figure murmured.

'That was kind of her,' he said with difficulty, 'but she did not understand. It is not my wish—' He stopped. 'That is—' He pulled himself together. 'You are kind and gracious, and I am sure you are very beautiful. Some man will be fortunate, but it cannot be me.'

The figure bent her head and raised her hands to cover her face.

'I beg you not to distress yourself,' Ali said gently. 'I must refuse this, because it would be a betrayal of the woman I love. That is something I can never do. Even on my wedding day, I shall not betray her in my heart. She'll never know that, nor will she care. But it will remain true, all my life.'

The figure lowered her hands from her face and held them clasped. Her head remained lowered, but her breast rose and fell as if from some violent emotion.

'Why do I tell you this?' Ali mused. 'Perhaps it's because you are a stranger and I cannot see your face that I can open my heart to you. I loved her, and I failed her—yes, truly, I did…' For the woman had shaken her head. 'When she was with me, there were many things I did not understand. Now it is too late.

'And so she left me, and I shall—' a shudder went through him '—shall never see her again. But she will live in my heart until my last breath. She is with me still, in every breeze that whispers. In the night her voice sings to me, in the morning her kiss awakens me. Her shadow will always be beside me.'

His voice had the quietness of heartbreak. The listening figure was very still, but in the flickering light from the lamp Ali saw a tear glistening on her cheek.

'Why do you weep?' he asked, taking a step towards her. 'Not for her. She is free of a man she couldn't love. Not for me, for I shall always have the joy of loving her.'

'Always?' the figure asked softly.

'Always, until I lie in my grave and she lies in hers, and the wind blows the sand to infinity, and there is no trace of our lives. Perhaps somewhere there is a garden where we shall meet again, without pain or misunderstanding. So you see, you must leave me, for I have nothing to offer.'

At last she raised her head.

'But I have not come to take,' she whispered. 'Only to give.'

Her veil fell. Ali stared in thunderstruck silence, then a glad cry broke from him.

'You!' he said. *'You!'*

The next moment Fran was in his arms, crushed by a kiss that felt like the first he had ever given her.

'You!' he said again. 'You all the time. You came back to me. But how——?'

This time Fran silenced him with lips that never spoke a word, yet told him all he wanted to know.

'How could I leave you?' she said at last. 'I thought I wanted to, but then you released me to marry Howard and I knew you loved me.'

'I have always loved you,' he said humbly. 'But I never learned how to ask, only to take. If not for you, I might have gone through life without knowing that the greatest prizes can only be won, not seized. But for your wisdom, my sweet life, we might have married and yet lost each other on our wedding day.

'Now we shall never lose each other, and our wedding day will be a time of joy and triumph. At least——' he checked himself '——I beg you to marry me...'

She smiled. 'Your mother is already arranging our wedding.'

'My mother——?'

'I telephoned her when you left me that day in England. She told me to fly out here, and arranged everything.'

'Then——you love me?' He said the words softly, as though he hardly dared to believe them. 'After everything I've done——how can you love me?'

'It's only now that I know how much I love you. Now that I can *be* myself, I can *give* myself. A prisoner has nothing to give. And I want to give only to you. But you must tell me something. You spoke of a woman you loved, but you didn't say her name. Tell me who you love.'

'Frances,' he said. 'It is Frances that I love. The others—' he gave a rueful smile '—perhaps they'll return sometimes, for you are a woman of variety, and will always have a new self to bemuse me. But it is Frances that I love, and always will.

'Be your true self. Come to me in freedom, and leave also in freedom, for I know—' his face darkened, as though it was hard for him to say this '—you will wish to return sometimes to your own country. As long as you always come back to me.'

'Always,' she said. 'Always. My darling, let us too build an Enchanted Garden.'

Looking into her eyes, he divined her true meaning.

'One that we shall carry with us all our lives,' he said, 'until the time comes for us to wander in the Enchanted Garden for ever.'

Tyler Brides

It happened one weekend...

Quinn and Molly Spencer are delighted to accept three bookings for their newly opened B&B, Breakfast Inn Bed, located in America's favorite hometown, Tyler, Wisconsin.

But Gina Santori is anything but thrilled to discover her best friend has tricked her into sharing a room with the man who broke her heart eight years ago....

And Delia Mayhew can hardly believe that she's gotten herself locked in the Breakfast Inn Bed basement with the sexiest man in America.

Then there's Rebecca Salter. She's turned up at the Inn in her wedding gown. Minus her groom.

Come home to Tyler for three delightful novellas by three of your favorite authors: Kristine Rolofson, Heather MacAllister and Jacqueline Diamond.

HARLEQUIN®
Makes any time special ™

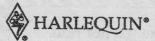

If you enjoyed what you just read,
then we've got an offer you can't resist!

Take 2 bestselling love stories FREE!
Plus get a FREE surprise gift!